About the Author

Niall McGrath is originally from County Antrim, Northern Ireland. He has been editor of a literary journal and literary arts administrator, among other professions. He has several volumes of poetry published in recent years. But his first love has always been fiction, which he is now concentrating on.

To: my late mother Olive

Niall McGrath

THE WAY OF TENDERNESS

AUSTIN MACAULEY
PUBLISHERS LTD.

A CIP catalogue record for this title is available from the British Library.

ISBN 9781785543791 (Paperback)
ISBN 9781785543807 (Hardback)
ISBN 9781785543814 (E-Book)

www.austinmacauley.com

First Published (2016)
Austin Macauley Publishers Ltd.
25 Canada Square
Canary Wharf
London
E14 5LQ

"Experience is as to intensity, not as to duration." (*Thomas Hardy*)

Chapter 1

Songhua Village, Jilin Province, China, November 1815

Lan watched from the tavern as the young village men carried An's bier from the temple courtyard and its temporarily, respectfully abandoned market stalls, up the nearest hill among the range of forest-covered hills, to the grave mound. The village drum tower was pealing mournfully; a lone boy walked before the funeral procession playing a sorrowful tune on a horn. Behind him, another carried a painting of a white haired and bearded old man, dressed in red and gold finery, sitting on an ornate throne: *Tu Di Gong*, the earth god. The sun was low in the winter sky as the bier was placed at its final resting place, on a platform of wood.

"Whose funeral is it?" the drunk customer asked her, looking through the open door, above which was nailed the sign, *House of the Way of Tenderness*. He was one of a pair of drovers, stopped for a bite to eat and a beer or two.

"The eunuch An."

The other drover scoffed. "They mourn a eunuch this much?! Look at that old fool!"

Ju embraced the corpse, kissed the cold cheek. The *tusi*, the village chief, made a brief speech. An's widow, Ai, was handed the burning torch. She touched the kindling beneath the body and the bier went up with a whoosh. It was beginning to rain and the flames were soon casting rainbow-hued sparks into the swirling air as smoke rose from the raging bier.

"Lady Ju was very fond of the eunuch An."

"Why?"

Lan shrugged her shoulders.

"Your Madame must have trusted him to serve her in other ways!" the drunk driver chortled. "Say, girlie," he tugged at her tunic, "How about coming to the room with me?"

"No room for you here!" she snatched his hand from her clothing. "This is a respectable house! That's one thing Lady Ju is most particular about!"

"Then why the name – *House of the Way of Tenderness*? Is that this street's name? Or surely …?"

"No, not that. I don't know, but it's not what you think, either. Drink up and go on your way!"

"Huh!" one drover said to the other, doing just that. "Let's press on to Jilin City. At least you can be sure of a wench there. What sort of place is this?"

As they stumbled off to round up their livestock, Lan looked out again at the sad occasion being played out a couple of hundred yards away. On the hilltop, Ju stood back as the flames rose. She threw petals onto the bier.

"Goodbye, dear An!"

Ju turned and walked away, head bowed. The aged Ning, braided hair queue grey between his shoulder blades, dressed in Manchu finery, followed at a respectful distance, nodding to the elders in acknowledgment of what he must do. He accompanied her down the path, towards the hostelry.

When they reached the tavern, Ju walked past Lan, straight to her rooms at the back. Ning removed his hat, set it on the bar, asked Lan for a drink. She poured and passed him a measure of beer.

"My lady Ju is distraught, Master Ning."

"Very much so. She is away to lie down. Her head aches." Ning sipped his beer as the thumping from the drum tower and horn accompaniment eased to an end. The roar of the pyre overwhelmed for a while. The villagers retreated from the hillside now, too.

"Our guests have gone?" Ning asked, seeing them in the distance with their straggle of goats and sheep.

"Drovers," Lan told him. "Rough sorts. There'd be fighting before long if they'd stayed."

"You're catching on quick to this trade."

Lan smiled proudly. Her pretty face radiated the attractiveness of youth.

"Li!" he exclaimed.

His drinking buddy, the grey-haired old fellow, had slipped away from the funeral party at Ai's home to share a beer with Ning here, in the room he found more congenial. Lan set the beer before Li.

"Why doesn't Lady Ju permit courtesans to ply their trade here?" Lan asked Ning, brushing against his thigh with casual familiarity.

"*I* don't. Nor she."

"Oh …"

"What?" As Lan poured him another beer, too, Ning probed, winking at Li, "Because I admire your youthful beauty, eye you up as any man would, because you sense I

3

wish you to be a concubine, which I might, but would never do, you wonder why I'm ascetic in attitude?"

Lan turned, washing the dishes left by the drovers. She shrugged her shoulders again. Her voice lowered almost to a whisper, her eyes rolled with coquettish allure as she said, "I have been told you are only half-Chinese, Master Ning." Slowly, she raised her face to stare into his light eyes daringly. "The *fanquis* have strange ways."

Li snorted. "You!" He pointed at Ning, red-faced. "A foreign devil?! The girl has the measure of you."

Ning patted Lan's bottom. "And best she doesn't forget it!" More seriously, he said to her, "Your place is secure here so long as you serve well, whether concubine or not, Lan. And, yes, I am a foreigner, a Boston man, an American. Turned native." Li nodded, grinning, enjoying Ning's sport with the girl, supping more beer. "Ning, who was once Nathan Gray. But it's not my Puritan upbringing, my innate Christian rectitude that renders me stuffy. Not when I am in the presence of such unutterable beauty as yours, Lan ..." For a moment, his hand rose, as if to cup a firm breast as hot as the pyre that glowed red on the hill, hesitated, then drifted back to rest on his knee. "Nor is it my unquenchable love and lust for our lady Ju that prevents me from permitting the pleasures of the flesh to be freely enjoyed in our tavern." He shook his head as he gulped down the rest of the latest pitcher of beer, his cheeks already flushing red. "It's a long, story, Lan. About how my *mother*," he almost spat out the word, "disappointed me. How I met Ju. Met!" he snorted, gulping more beer that Lan poured him from a huge jug. "Travelled with her on the winding path that led us here, to the *Way of Tenderness*. How she, An, his poor now widow Ai, Li, how all of us became *jiaren*, extended family, a household together. What it all *means*. If you, or I for that matter, or any one can work out what it all means. This crazy experience called life." He laughed, practically hysterically. "All starting with An saving my life."

"Is that why Lady Ju revered the eunuch?" Lan asked, gazing out as the sun set and the fire burned orange and scarlet against a pink horizon. The moon was already in the sky, full and huge, looming eerily.

He shook his head, also staring out at the funeral pyre. "There is so much more to it than merely that. Isn't that right, Li?"

Li nodded. "I have heard some of the tale. And I was there for some of it."

At the drum tower, the local lad tolled the drum one last peal and silently descended, as darkness fell upon Songhua. And Ju slept with the tears dried upon her eyes as Ning recounted to Lan and Li their sad, passionate, convoluted history.

Chapter 2

South China Sea, Autumn 1776

Firestorm pitched violently to port and Nathan tiptoed involuntarily across the wardroom like a dancer stepping out across the stage as the melody of *Swan Lake* rises to a crescendo. Although he had not experienced this before, he realised the thunderous roars were canon blasts. Nathan gasped at the ship's horse-like resistance and the creaking of timbers around him.

He did not have time to wonder about why *Firestorm* was so suddenly engaged in some kind of firing exercise. His morning rounds as officer of the watch were forgotten as sailors darted past him. Leading hands screamed at their men, most of whom were only half-ready, many with patches in their striped trousers and grubby white shirts being haphazardly buttoned as they hurried to the upper deck.

Nathan realised he should be at the Captain's side and so gripped at a wooden rail, hauled himself to the ladder and fought against the cabin boy to scale it. They both reached the balmy air together. Nathan was catapulted by a jolt of the ship, forward and face downwards. There was a tremendous explosion of splinters, smoke and the rotten-egg stench of black powder.

When Nathan picked himself up off the wooden planks, his hand was wet. He saw it was blood, not water. Then, he saw the remains of the cabin boy bundled against the bulkhead, butchered flesh and bone in rags. The wooden cage of chickens that was being aired on the upper deck was in pieces, the hens all dead. A pig had got loose and was squealing its mad way, weaving in panic through the hand-to-hand fighting men.

Instinctively, Nathan shouted at an elderly seaman, "Simeon, where's the captain?"

The man pointed for'ard. Stooping as a wave of salty water crashed over him, Nathan balanced himself as he jogged forwards to the captain's side.

"What's going on, sir?"

"Pirates. Came out of nowhere!"

The *Firestorm*'s canon blasted again in series, each firing raising her until she would rock back down onto the mirror-smooth South China Sea.

Nathan half-saw more bodies leap across from the other ship's side, the Oriental sailors swarming suddenly like insects onto *Firestorm*. Sailors held cutlasses against the onslaught. He heard the scrape of steel on steel, the squeals as men were pierced and abruptly died. As the canon-smoke clawed at the back of his throat, making him sneeze mucus over his shirt and retch, clutching his belly, Nathan knew only that sheer animal instinct must have compelled him back down the ladder. He tried to unsheathe his short sword, sensing the danger close behind. A long, loud grunting like a pig was bearing down on him, the damp heat of breath was literally on his neck. A weight knocked him over, pinned him down.

Nathan's fingers scraped the timbers for his sword. The weight disappeared and he turned, scrabbled away with his heels, against the wooden bulkhead, and gripped the sword, prodding it in front of him, his vision blurred with panic.

He realised it was the tubby Han pantry hand, An, a few feet away, slashing at the scrawny pirate with a cleaver. Nathan felt the warmth of blood spotting his cheek and lips. He turned his face from the onslaught as the bulky eunuch grunted with each blow he chopped into flesh and bone. Staggering to his feet again, he brushed at the red spots on his white shirt, stockings and beige trousers, so that they smeared pink. His eyes stared into An's, bewilderment and shock evident in that gaze. In return, An's eyes twinkled as his huge mouth spread broadly with a wicked grin.

"Close, sir!" An called.

Nathan nodded. The ship pitched as it roared again and, without discussion, they bounced with the ship, scaling the ladder again to the upper deck. Fearlessly, An threw open the wooden hatch doors and pounced forward, snarling and brandishing his cleaver. Nathan bolted out in quick succession, sword at the ready.

To his surprise, the pirates were in retreat. Their main sail was afire. An chased a pirate to the edge of *Firestorm*'s deck. The gap between the two ships was too great now for the Chinese pirate to jump. He leapt anyway and splashed into the sea below.

Nathan rushed for'ard again, to Captain Hearty's side. Men were firing muskets at the retreating brigand. The captain was shouting orders to cease firing the canon.

"They've given up?"

"A tactical retreat, perhaps, to lick their wounds," he told Nathan, his Dorset burr reassuring. "Hopefully, before they have recovered we'll be in safer waters, beyond Canton. They got so close out of the fog, they managed to block our canon ports. But we got a few flaps open when she hove to."

"But my father's ship is behind us by a few hours, they may be in danger?"

Joseph shrugged his shoulders. "They don't know the *Firepower*'s coming. Besides, he can take care of himself. Once again, we live to make it to Canton, to sell our cargo and take aboard our consignment of tea."

"You've faced this kind of thing before?"

"Occupational hazard for a trader in this world."

"This is a different world?" Nathan stared at his father's old friend without being able to mask his worried expression.

The captain laughed heartily.

Routine in the *Firestorm* was settled again when, a couple of hours after the encounter with the pirate vessel, Nathan finished his watch on the bridge and descended to his shared cabin. Men were scrubbing away the blood from outside the wardroom passageway where, earlier, An had butchered the pirate.

As he passed, a seaman on his knees scrubbing, his back to Nathan, moved his leg and half-tripped him up. Nathan struck the man a blow across the back of the head and shoulders with his arm and wrist. He felt the blow himself, but stifled any reaction.

"Watch out!" he growled.

The man rose on his knees, faced him. "Pardon, sir!" he barked, tugging at an invisible forelock.

Nathan nodded back, carried on, on his way.

Before he went to his cabin, though, he turned in at the wardroom pantry. Li, the cook was busy at the oven, baking bread. The pantry hand was not there.

"Where's your man?"

"Off watch, sir. I can …"

Nathan shook his head. He hesitated a moment, then said, "That big eunuch is a clumsy oaf most of the time, but this afternoon he did me a great favour. He helped me tackle a pirate that had got inside the ship. Good show."

"Sir." Nodding, the cook smiled as he lowered his head to his work, kneading dough on the flour-dusted bench before him again, relieved and pleasantly surprised by the unexpected praise.

Midshipman Gray was not aware of it, but the big eunuch was just through the opening, in the passageway, listening with a grin. All the same, An sidled away and out of sight before the Boston gentleman left the galley.

Nathan went to the cabin he shared with seven other officers. They had four bunks between them, not hammocks like the men, which they shared in pairs, having access to one when their opposite numbers were on watch and they were off. He removed his braided jacket, loosened his shirt at the neck and eased his back onto the rough straw mattress. It was warm, for someone had just gone on watch. Across the *grot*, snoring from behind a modesty curtain that was draped over another of the bunks. Nathan felt a weight bear down on him as he lay flat on his back, boots propped up on the wooden bunk-end.

Eyes closed, his head swirled. Exhaustion overwhelmed him for some minutes. He could feel the tiredness flow from his body in waves.

Nathan was back in Boston, a few years ago. At the end of the dinner table, in his father's house, sitting beside his school friend, James Otis III, whose father was also there. Joseph Hearty was one of the men round the table. There was tension in the atmosphere at tonight's dinner. Their elders were discussing the Stamp Act.

"The *Dartmouth*'s on its way, full to the gills with tea," Adam Gray was commenting to Otis. "What does brother Adams propose we do?"

"A tax is a tax, in any man's language. It's an affront to our rights, our self-determination."

Gray lowered his head. "We're a colony."

"Do we have to be?" Otis demanded.

There was a murmur of "Hear hear," around the table.

Gray looked up. "Are you a son of liberty?"

Otis stared him in the eye. "I am."

Gray nodded. "I reckon it's close to being time to make a stand."

Otis bellowed, "Haven't we already done so, at Adams' meeting at the Hall. We passed the resolution, that the *Dartmouth* will be sent back, vile levy unpaid."

Gray shrugged his shoulders. "What is needed is action."

"That, too," Otis affirmed. "Twenty-five sentries have been appointed this night to ensure no tea is unloaded."

"The Governor is expecting the duty to be paid, even if that occurs."

Otis bellowed, "Damn his tax! He won't get a penny."

James and Nathan had waited until their fathers and their friends were in the drawing room, smoking and drinking, before sneaking from the house. As they were passing through the hall, Nathan's mother noticed him and went over to him.

"Is your father still talking rot and politics in the drawing room?"

Nathan laughed. "He is, mother!"

"What?" she defended her stance. "God will resolve it all."

"God helps those who help themselves," young Otis told her.

"James, you're a feisty youth," she said to him. "Well, let's hope this trouble comes to a speedy end."

"Yes, ma'am," James placated her.

When she had turned her back and returned to her lady guests, the two boys slipped out of the house. Down at the harbour, the night time wharves were not their usual quiet selves: men with burning torches, dressed in native animal skins, faces painted like Mohawks, were milling on the jetty before the three ships. The officer of the watch and captain of the *Dartmouth* were remonstrating with some of the vocal leaders of the demonstration.

"Damn your taxable tea!" someone roared.

The shoving and pushing meant that more men ebbed forward, up the gangway. Sailors appeared on deck. They were swept aside by a sudden surge.

Nathan grabbed one lad by the jacket. "What's happening, George?"

"See for yourself!" he shouted, freeing himself to rush aboard and join in the melee. His comrades had joined the crowd on the deck, who were emptying tea crates, letting the black gold they held spill over the side and into the still, moon-mirrored water. It swooshed as delicately as silk into the dark North Atlantic.

James held on to Nathan's jacket so hard he was hauling his shoulder down. "We're in trouble now."

Nathan jerked free. "Huh. Damn the Limeys."

"Midshipman Gray!"

Nathan sat up with a start. It was Joseph. "Captain Hearty ..." he began to struggle to his feet.

A hand pressed his knee. "Relax, lad. It's your rest time. No, I just wanted a few words with you."

Nathan was sitting propped up on the bunk on an elbow as his superior officer perched on the opposite bunk, as if the wooden lip of it were a shooting stick. It was unusual for the captain to come to the men's *grots*, even an officer's, except when carrying out an inspection. He did not want to be accused of favouritism. Nor did he feel comfortable being close to Joseph because he was his father's friend and he felt a certain insecurity around him, an uncharacteristic lack of confidence that disturbed him.

"I've had run-ins with pirates before, but make no mistake, Nathan, that was by far the closest shave."

Nathan started so that the bunk trembled. "Really?"

"Hm, they don't usually get aboard. For a wee while there, I thought it was touch and go, they were going to overwhelm us. A good lesson for one as young as yourself, dealing with that. And you acquitted yourself with aplomb, rooting out that weasel who got below decks. Now, before long we will reach Canton where we'll meet up with your father's ship. Before we do so, there are a few things I need to make you aware of.

"The Chinese trade like us, indeed they are perhaps even better organised administratively than us. Partly an admirable thing, but also annoying. The damned bureaucracy, I mean. Also, they take things a bit slower than us, mark the simplest of things with an element of ritual."

"Like the tea drinking ceremony?"

"Exactly, lad. All that palaver over just a sup of tea. Anyway, I guess we're just a young nation on the rise and on the make, whereas they are a centuries-old country and have all the time in the world to … take their time."

"The Americas are hardly a nation, sir."

"I got a letter from home – sounds like there may have been trouble brewing."

Nathan's brow furrowed. "Really? But ... won't the English ...?"

"God knows how it will all end. What they'll do, dream up next from that rotten little island of theirs."

"Your home, sir!"

"I was born there, reared there, and pressed into service there, pretty damn smart. Naw. Out here, on the ocean, this is the only real home I've known so far."

"May God be with us."

Joseph Hearty nodded. "Let's hope luck is on our side, too. Anyway, it shouldn't affect our trading here. The Chinese don't care and the English ships aren't men-o-war. But, my point is, also, the Chinese ... they've been around for many a moon and, well, we might think ourselves Christians and they heathens and all that, but, they tend to look down on us."

He saw in Nathan's face the expected tightening that meant he was surprised, affronted, angered.

"They've been civilised for centuries, even back when our kind were in the Dark Ages in Europe and quite savage. Ports, of course, tend also to be at times brutal places. Sailors drink, there are the opium dens. The Chinese see these as a scourge *we've* brought to them."

"We have a load of opium aboard, sir."

Joseph bowed his head, as if ashamed to admit to it. "It's a legal cargo. We trade freely, that's the principle on which commerce operates. Physicians do use it. We can't know who's buying the stuff, where it's destined. Anyway," he squeezed Nathan's knee again as he rose to his feet, reminding him of his junior position, "Nathan, you just need a wee bit of an open mind and a bit of discretion sometimes, dealing with the men and others ashore. Mostly, the place is civilised. But, being sailors, sometimes we encounter the seedier side of life."

"Is Canton worse than the seedy side of Boston?"

"What do you know of the seedy side of Boston, lad?"

"Not a lot at all!" Nathan laughed.

"Glad to hear it! Well, anyway, pre-warned is pre-armed and all that. Be careful."

"Yes, Captain."

"Get some rest."

"Yes, Captain!" As Hearty left, Nathan lay back on the bunk. But at the doorway as Joseph Hearty left he heard a mutter and the captain speak back kindly to someone. Nathan looked up to see the bulk of An the eunuch in the *grot*. He propped himself up again, on his stiff elbow.

"What do you want?" he growled.

An offered him a handleless cup of steaming green tea, on a saucer. Nathan took it, thanking him. Without another word, the kitchen hand departed. Nathan stared after him, realising it was a thank you gift, and relieved he had accepted it graciously, rather than barking at him to take it away, he did not want anything, which is how he really felt. Nathan took a couple of sips, though he preferred his tea black, with milk, the European way. It was too hot but pleasantly sweet.

Chapter 3

Songhua Village, Jilin Province, China, Autumn 1776

Ju was in the tea field with her father, Jia. Her sister was getting married this Harvest Moon Festival, so the others were busy making rice cakes, lanterns and working on the thousand other preparations for Mei's betrothal. But her brother, Dewei, had turned an ankle, could hardly stand, so the rangy, nineteen year old Ju was out on the land, among the rows of bushes, helping to harvest the last, late corner of crop.

"I can manage on my own, Ju."

"Father, many hands make light work. We'll be twice as quick together!" she beamed, her Nankeen breeches and blouse becoming green-stained from her rubbing against the branches in the rows as she picked the tea leaves from the plants. Her hands were red-raw as she worked. Jia admired the expression of determination on his daughter's face as she seized the tender leaves, tore them from their stalks, wiped the sweat from her brow, and ignored the stinging of her palms and fingers. She would make some man a good wife. Pride pulsed through his veins. He stared up at the lowering sun that was about to sink beneath a cloudbank, felt the gentle breeze on his cheeks and thanked the moon goddess Chang'e, who would be making her appearance soon from behind the mountains, that he was blessed with such fine children.

They were all sturdy, loyal, hard-working, and honest. And they were all obedient, except for Ju. Her self-reliance only made her more admirable, he realised, for that streak of independence was a sign of strength. Perhaps, also, though he scarcely dared recognise it, she was much like himself. Her mother would, no doubt, agreed that his own wilfulness was reflected in Ju's quiet confidence. She had been one of twin girls, unfortunately her other half had died a couple of days after the birth. Ju had been a runt, but a survivor. There was an inner strength that he believed made her indefatigable.

Jia recalled the time when Heng was expecting Dewei. He had to deliver a load of tea to Jilin City. He brought the toddler Ju with him, to give the heavily pregnant woman some peace in her confinement, and to allow the other women to concentrate on the new arrival. As the convoy of carts sauntered along the road, each donkey tied to the back of another's cart, and the other two men from the village who were going with them slept in the last cart, on top of the sacks of pungent black, dried leaves, little Ju sat up front with her father, singing her lungs out.

When they had got to Jilin, it was already dark. They had found a buyer for their tea and a stable for their donkeys and carts for the night and had gone into town to find somewhere to eat. In the bustle of the noisy street, Ju had suddenly darted off, between someone's legs and away from him. Jia had called after her, searching frantically for a short time. Then he saw her, leaning against a doorpost, staring in at a band as they played and sang in the posh restaurant.

"You want to hear a band?" he laughed. "Not this one. We wouldn't be allowed in this restaurant," he told her.

"Why not?" Her question went unanswered as Jia led her by the hand to the tavern where their companions were already downing beer.

"You found the scamp!" they greeted Jia.

Food was brought, beer for him, and they sat with the tiny Ju transfixed as the less-accomplished musician there played song after song.

Jia and Ju picked and basketed the last of the tea crop for this year and made their way wearily back to the house. It was just a short walk past the shelter of the trees and the pigsty, across the open yard to the plain building. As they passed the long window in the gable wall with a shutter propped up, they could hear Mei and her mother arguing about the colour of dress Heng might wear. At the front, they removed their dusty boots before going up the two wooden steps onto the veranda. Little Hua was standing at the table on the veranda, kneading dough on a flour-covered bread board.

"Making cakes for me?" Jia laughed, seizing Hua and lifting the ten-year-old into the air.

Hua struggled, shrieked. "Yah! You're sweaty!"

He set her down. Ju went on into the room she shared with Hua. She peeled off her blouse and washed at the jug and bowl on the dresser. The cold water made her flesh goose bump. When she was clean, Ju eased her hips from the breeches and wiped her feet dry with a towel. She took a fresh, blue cotton dress from a wooden chest and slipped it on.

Instead of joining her mother and sister in the kitchen, Ju went outside, slipping on her sandals at the veranda.

"Where are you going?" Hua asked.

She passed her sister and went on, ignoring the question. Ju walked along the dry path through the white pear grove. She plucked a fruit from a branch as she passed and bit into its succulent, energy-reviving flesh as she strolled the short distance to the cluster of houses and stalls that were the village. To one side of the built-up place, the road extended up the hill, past Madame Lihwa's ramshackle old tavern to the grave mound. The other fork at the end of the village wound past tall poplars and willows by the lake and river to the drum tower and temple beyond. Ju smiled and said hello to Gui's mother, who was carrying a pitcher of beer home from the tavern for her husband and herself. Ju turned along the other path, made her way past the trees.

At the end of the planting, where the rhododendron bushes cast multi-coloured petals upon the grass and emitted a heady aroma, Gui and his sister Guan-yin were waiting. A quick bounce across the wood and rope bridge over the river to the drum tower and the three got the communal instruments from their trunks, beneath benches.

Unlike many drum towers, this one did not protrude from among a cluster of low roofs. It nestled near the steep rock-face of one of the near hills, surrounded by fruit trees, with the river mouth and lake winding by. The pagoda layers stepped up in decreasing rows towards the pinnacle from its octagonal base structure, to a height of almost seventy feet. The veranda commanded pleasant views of the village and lake. But the village's rural location and relative poverty were evident in the ragged appearance: roof shingles were loose, veranda timbers were warped, and some ornamentation had been nipped off by winter winds as if some gigantic gardener had only half-heartedly deadheaded a rhododendron bush. The interior decorations, carved ornaments, lanterns and temple-like accoutrements were dusty, dull, and tired-looking. It was always cool inside, whatever the temperature outside.

19

Gui lifted one of the strapped double-drums and began intoning a rapid beat on it, as if it were an Indian *mirdanga*. Guan-yin was soon accompanying him on a *banhu*. Its string tones mesmerised Ju's consciousness like the voice of a siren. She closed her eyes, swayed her head, before accompanying them on the brass and wood horn.

Guan-yin began to sing. Between horn phrases, Ju joined in. Gui added his deeper voice to the harmony. The effort warmed them physically as well as taking their minds off the chilly interior of the vast, high space with its floor above that housed the three huge, red-sided, skin-covered drums that were the pride of Songhua and which now, only on special occasions, intoned the time.

Old Duyi had wandered over from his cabin, shuffling with a dragon-headed walking stick. He sat on a bench, face transformed by the tune, silhouetted against the lattice of window slits behind him.

When the youngsters paused for breath, he clapped. "Ah, you don't need any practice. You should be in a competition, like the Provincial Contest in Jilin."

"Really?" Ju was taken aback.

"Are we good enough for that?" Gui exclaimed.

"Certainly! Might as well give it a bash! Bit of adventure, rather than being stuck here in sleepy Songhua all your time."

"Did you ever go to Jilin, Duyi?"

"Of course, Guan-yin! Many times. And many other cities. But not recently. When the bones get tired, and you get short of puff, you can't be bothered with the dash and pace of busy towns."

"Sounds exciting!" Gui said to Ju as Duyi raised his frail frame and said his goodbyes.

"I wonder, *could* we compete in the contest?" Ju asked her friends.

Gui told her, "I'll ask our father first. He'll be most amenable, of them all. He might be able to persuade your parents to let you go, then, too."

"It's a calm afternoon, want to go a quick splash out on the lake in the boat?" Guan-yin suggested.

"Hasn't Ju to help with Mei's wedding preparations?"

She shrugged her shoulders. "It's all done now."

So they made their way to the sloping grass bank where the boats were tied to stakes.

"It's too calm to fish," Guan-yin told them.

They set off on the rippling water, Guan-yin manning the oars first. Ju sat beside Gui on the cold wooden plank. Their thighs sat alongside, touching when the boat gently bobbed from side to side as Guan-yin pulled on the oars.

"Lovely dress," Gui commented, running the back of his fingers along the cotton at the shoulder, until they lingered on her bare arm-top for a moment. Ju's eyes widened with embarrassment, looking to make sure his sister was intent on her rowing and did not notice this intimacy.

"It's for tomorrow. But I was too eager to try it on."

"Beautiful. As if you have been dipped in the sky."

"You're a poet, Gui. You could help me improve the lyrics of my songs."

"Ah, your songs are excellent!"

"We might make a good song-writing team, Gui," Ju had enthused before she knew what was coming out of her mouth.

"It's getting darker," Guan-yin said. A blast of cold air encircled them as it suddenly arrived over the mountains and vortexed around them. In the distance, the treetops all danced as the breeze built up.

Without mentioning it, Gui took over rowing and began heading back to the drum tower. They were quite a way out, before long the wind was sweeping rain against them. Some leaves reached them from the far shore. Gui's arms were beginning to tire. Ju moved beside him and took one of the oars. Their thighs touched again; again the heat through cloth. But this time there was not time to ponder the ecstasy of closeness: they were struggling to force the craft homewards.

By the time they were near the shore, the surface was chopped up by gusts. The boat was bucking like an irate Billy goat. Ju's oar slipped, the boat spun. When it settled, Gui cried aloud, Guan-yin was out!

The squall drove the boat into a tangle of bank branches where willows stood like sentries along the edge of Madame Lihwa's smallholding. Gui dragged Ju from the boat, through muck, roots and stinging weeds towards the house there. Lihwa saw them approach her door, let them in. Helped them dry themselves.

"Guan-yin!" Gui shrieked over and over, standing in the garden, looking out over the lake, getting soaked again. His sister was nowhere to be seen. Ju ran to rouse help. Men came, with poles, one with a spyglass. They scoured the banks. Gui's father and brothers came running. As the hours passed and the half-storm passed, Gui fell asleep on a mat on Lihwa's floor. Ju lay beside him for warmth, wide awake, praying for a miracle.

It was Jia who came. By the time he did so, Ju was cowering foetally, whining like a wounded hound. "It was her own idea. It wasn't my fault. She and Gui made me go!"

Grabbing her arm and hauling her to her feet, Jia hissed in her ear, "Stop this nonsense, do you want people to think I beat you?"

Jia led her home, trancelike, to her mother's arms. There, just in through the door from the veranda, she broke down as her head squeezed against Heng's bosom.

Chapter 4

Pearl River, China, Autumn 1776

For the final run into their destination, Nathan had been rowed across from the *Firestorm* to the *Firepower*. Macao was the first port of call as the Yellow Sea narrowed to the Bogue, the so-called *'tiger's mouth'* of the Pearl River that led to Canton – or Guangzhou to the locals. The land between the many defensive forts that protected this valuable trading place was bright with Red Silk Cotton trees aflower and colourful orange groves, but it was the throngs of vessels of all sizes bobbing in and out of the Bogue estuary that amazed Nathan. Boston seemed a provincial backwater compared with this noisy, busy place. He stared in amazement as Chinese sailors ploughed their fishing junks, as well as international schooners and trading brigantines, back and forth to Macao and Hong Kong in the distance across the vast bay.

His father was hanging on to a rope, face red with pride and excitement. "We made it, boy. Isn't it marvellous, Nathan – China lies before us!"

He nodded, trying to hide worry. "Amazing, Captain. Has to be seen to be believed. Makes home look small."

"Organised chaos, lad!" Captain Gray murmured, before bellowing orders to the men atop.

With the wind on his face, the briny smell mingling with smoke and unknown smells from bankside factories, canteens and warehouses in his nostrils, Nathan grinned, coming to terms with impending adventure.

Nathan was ordered to accompany the captain in the boat when he was rowed across from the *Firepower*, anchored along with the other vessels in Macao Roads, to that first port itself. His father led Nathan from the harbour wall to a long office building with a Chinese scripted sign above the door. Nathan noted in his mind that this building had a high, ornate sandstone façade. It was as impressive as any public building in Massachusetts.

"Customs?"

"Chophouse!" Robert Gray was delirious as a child on Christmas morning.

Nathan frowned. He had not been told what any of this meant. He followed dutifully, removing his cap as they entered. They went to a table where an official was seated. The suited Oriental fellow filled in two forms with a quill. Robert Gray told him the ships' names, which he inscribed in the appropriate places. Hearing the names of the ships, the fellow smiled, made a chuckling sound, and became momentarily excited. He gabbled something to Adam, who grinned broadly. The captain signed the two forms. The official stamped them with a wax seal and handed them to him.

"You know the rules at Whampoa?" He did not even wait for Adam to confirm. "The Eight Regulations are posted at factory. Do not rove about the bays selling goods to rascals or deal with smugglers," he tried to read from a script before him. "No womens, guns, spears or arms of any kind at factory. Do not row about Yellow River in own boat seeking pleasure. Is permitted go to Temple to pray to

Buddha, to stroll in flower gardens, three days per month only, but in droves of less than ten at a time. All visits cease before nightfall, no foreign devils ashore passing night in Canton or carousing together when dark, and disturbing native good peoples. You know?"

Adam nodded vigorously. "Same as before."

The official pointed to two seamen waiting nearby. Robert took some money from his pocket and handed an equal share to each man. They all moved outside.

"The Canton System," he explained to his son. "This is the chop," he handed the piece of paper to Nathan. "Don't lose it."

"A permit?"

Robert nodded. "These are our pilots. After we've got on *Firepower,* you go on to *Firestorm* with your man."

Before he left them, Adam spoke excitedly to the two pilots in their own language. They produced red, white and blue folded cloth bundles. Nathan wondered what the hubbub was about. His father seemed agitated, but was giving nothing away. He seemed to be giving the locals some instruction.

Nathan asked the pilot, "Do you know any English?"

"Oh, I know English well."

"What's your name, man?"

"I am Kangxi, Mister Nathan."

"Very good, Kangxi. Named after the Emperor?"

The man smiled and nodded.

They got back into their waiting boat and were rowed back to their ships.

Just as Captain Gray was getting up to follow the pilot up the crawl net to *Firepower*'s deck, steadying himself as the boat rocked beneath their feet, Nathan asked him, "What next?"

"Through the end of this Bogue estuary, up the Pearl River, then we get inspected."

"What for?"

"The Canton System: they note how many men we have on board, how many guns, our cargo."

"Nosy beggars."

Captain Gray shrugged his shoulders, "When in Rome. Then, these fellows leave and the river pilots come aboard."

"More expense. I'm getting to understand their system."

The captain nodded knowingly. "And we get our Hong merchant then. We have to let him take his pick of merchandise. Sing-songs. Wind up clocks, they usually go for. Mind and tell Joseph, no more than one big crate! Then on to Jackass Point and Whampoa Island at Canton." Robert sliced the air with a vertical hand, excited by arriving at the trading station. "So, son, see you at the factory."

"Factory?" Nathan called up the net, but his father did not hear him. He was already climbing over the wooden rail and onto the deck of his command.

"The warehouse you are appointed to," Kangxi told him with his usual grin. "You are factors. It is a factory. Controlled by the Hong merchant in your honour. You sell through it. You travel in country, purchase next cargo, Hong merchant supply it and secure it through storage at factory until ready to sail. Then he give you the Grand Chop, permission to sail with goods legitimate."

"I'm beginning to see why China is such a rich trading nation," Nathan commented.

"Canton System developed over two thousand years of trading with the West," Kangxi informed Nathan, who detected the hint of sarcasm in the official's tone.

Nathan's silent expression conveyed the called-for amount of awe.

There was one more surprise for him. When they got to the ship, Kangxi had spoken animatedly with Joseph, who had nodded profusely. And when the two ships had taken on their river pilots and were approaching Whampoa and Canton, Nathan noticed that Joseph and Adam had both ships piped simultaneously, and the cry went up, "All hands on deck!"

At first he wondered was it some sort of attack. The bundle the pilot had brought had been given to the Hand of the Watch, who went to the aft mast. The two captains addressed the ships' companies at the same time.

They could not hear Captain Adam telling the *Firepower* crew the same thing, but Captain Joseph gave *Firestorm*'s men the news. "Men, it appears while we have been at sea, there has been a spot of bother at home. We are no longer subjects of the British Crown." As he told them this, the English ensign was being lowered, the man attached the new flag and the Stars and Stripes were raised in its place. "Independence has been declared. We are now free citizens of an American Republic! God bless America!" Someone began playing *The Marseillaise*. Both ships' companies gave three cheers and threw their caps in the air. Captain Joseph ordered an extra ration of rum for every man.

As they glided past the British factory and its fluttering Union Flag, Joseph muttered to Nathan, wiping tears from his cheeks with a grimy rag, "No more of that old Butcher's Apron for us, lad!" They moored alongside the factory with the Stars and Stripes on the flagpole before it, to the cheers of the men ashore from the other ship that was already there, Astor's *Magdalen*.

That evening, they welcomed their fellow Americans aboard for a celebration. Someone procured Chinese fireworks, let them off at midnight, so that multi-coloured sparks twinkled in the frosty air around the vast, nine-storey brick pagoda and above the ships as they danced gently on the calm waters of the harbour at Whampoa Island.

Chapter 5

Jilin City, Jilin Province, China, Autumn 1776

Gui was concentrating intently on his drumming in the dim, dingy bar, which had its name over the door painted on a weathered, wooden board in the narrow, bustling, roasted grains-stinking street outside: *Inn of the Way of Happiness*. It had an eerie echo around the tables since it was virtually empty. Just the owner puffing away at one table on an opium pipe. Ju closed her eyes to play the tune with greater feeling on the horn. She realised the drumming had ceased. Opening her eyes, she saw Gui had ceased because the owner had his hand in the air.

"These provincial melodies are fine as background music, but does the girl sing?"

Gui and Ju swapped an expectant glance for a moment. He began a mournful rhythm and Ju soon began to sing what would have been Guan-yin's part. Again, she closed her eyes, as if searching in some other dimension for the lyrics and for the right tone to convey the sorrow of the traditional song.

When they finished, the owner set the pipe from his lips. He nodded thoughtfully. "How many songs do you know?"

Gui replied, "Sixteen, sir."

"That'll do to begin with, for the first night. Try tomorrow, see how it goes. After that, if you stay, you'll need to know a few more."

"I've written a few of my, our own, sir," Ju blurted.

He dismissed them with a wave. "We'll come back to those in time if you stay."

As they left the bar, Gui stared at Ju. Reaching the street, he whispered, "What songs?"

She shrugged her shoulders. "Just some ideas I've had. I've one about Guan-yin ..." her voice cracked.

Gui put his arm around her shoulders. The drum swung, pressing them closer together. "It was an ill wind that took her from us. But, being banished for a while here to Jilin has been no bad thing – we can earn a little at this and maybe other places, and practice for the contest next month. But, you are upset, Ju. Let's get back to the room."

"We should go to the park and practise."

Gui pressed his mouth on hers. Ju did not kiss him back. She stared into his earnest eyes as he pleaded gently, "Let's go back awhile."

Ju hugged him momentarily, then freed herself from his grasp. "I care about you as a friend, Gui. Don't try to tempt me like that. It would spoil things between us. I can't think of you like that."

He followed her for a few steps. She turned and held out her arms. "Please don't hate me, Gui."

He shook his head. "I'll never do that. I'll always care about you. But don't worry, I'm not going to bother you ever again. I understand."

31

Ju smiled at him kindly. "I understand boys, I think. Don't worry, we'll find you a pretty Jilin girl!"

Gui beamed and hurried with her laughing on their way to the park to practise their songs.

"You've a beautiful voice," the man crooned.

He had appeared beside Ju when she went to the bar for a glass of water.

"Thank you," she said politely, quickly eyeing him up and down. Slightly flustered, she walked with him to his table as his drinks were brought to his couple of friends.

"Where are you from?"

"Songhua. A village."

He nodded. "I'm a city boy. Jilin born and bred. Isn't that right, Tengfei?"

His friend nodded, smiled, returned to make doe-eyes at the young woman beside him.

"I sing, too," he commented. "Perhaps you've heard of me? I'm Peng. And you are?"

Ju sucked in a breath in surprise. Peng was the top billing on Friday and Saturday evenings. He sang in this little place, she knew, because he got his start here. But he had engagements often in Dandong and other cities. He was usually touring. His songs were famous, even in Songhua. Ju's head spun a little, she had not expected to be sitting chatting with someone like him.

Ju was glad she had dressed up this week, their fourth week here. Changyin, the beautician from the building they rented the room in, had lent her a stage costume, one of the hairdresser's best outfits. The sleeves billowed light blue from the shoulders and down the back almost to the backs of the knees; a pale purple bodice was fastened at the neck by a criss-cross white cotton strap around the neck; the pleats across the bosom were pulled up between the breasts and lined with silver tassels, set off with a large sapphire-style stone; a few inches of material hung across the stomach but the midriff and navel were bare; a silver belt with stone-decorated tassels at the hip held up a deeper purple taffeta skirt. Ju's black hair was braided up in an elaborate bun at the back, with a silver clip holding her side parting, while the rest cascaded to her shoulders at the back. Coloured stone earrings matched her belt *accoutrements*. Her young cheeks gleamed white beneath a conservative brush of make-up, while her lips shone crimson. The fire of innocence burned in those fathomless, rock pool eyes.

Ju saw Gui sitting at the bar, chatting with that dancer Daiyu, glancing over occasionally as if to disapprove of her speaking with these people. Did he know who this was? Was he jealous, that Ju had managed to make such a potentially important contact?

"I hope you don't mind that I sing your song to myself, *Sorrow of the Roc*. It reminds me of my friend, Guan-yin."

"Are you close pals?" Peng tittered.

Ju blushed. "I'm a small village girl …"

"So?" Tengfei laughed, elbowing Ai, whom he always had by his side.

"She drowned," Ju explained.

Peng leaned forward, his touch lingering on Ju's arm. "My poor dear. To lose someone so close, so young. How awful for you. I lost a friend at your age, killed by a horse." He shook his head, remembering.

Ju felt embraced by his spirit. The hand slid casually from her covered arm to the bare flesh at the rise of her hip. She was wary, but instantly felt that she wanted to be daring.

"Are you touring again soon, Peng?" she asked.

"We travel in a few weeks' time. Songyuan, Beicheng, Changchun, Siping, Lioyuan, Baishan, maybe as far south as Tonghua."

"Wow! Great! How many go?"

"Sixteen. We have a full company. Maybe if you gain a name for yourself in the meantime, you can be in a touring company soon, Ju."

"Really?"

Peng nodded at Gui. "Your boyfriend is a superb musician and you sing so well."

"Oh, Gui's not my boyfriend, just …"

"A brother?" Tengfei asked.

Ju shook her head. "Well, like one, I guess. Actually, he is Guanyin's brother."

"A chaperone," Peng smiled.

"I don't need one of those!" Ju retorted.

They all laughed heartily. Ju was offered a puff on Tengfei's opium pipe. He made Ai show her it was fine. Ai obliged, though her body language betrayed discomfort. Ju tried it when Gui was busy talking intently to Daiyu, and as Tengfei was busy mauling his possession, Ai.

When Peng's party were leaving, Ju rose with them and walked with them, Peng's arm around her waist. She realised what was happening, made no decision to avoid it. She went with them to Peng's house in a rickshaw.

It was a luxurious city apartment. Once there, Tengfei began puffing on his pipe once more. But also he struck up a tune on a *banhu*. Ju's eyes filled with tears as Peng sat singing his solemn lament that reminded her of Guan-yin's last fateful trip on the lake. Seeing her weeping, Peng moved beside her when the song was over and embraced her. Soon, she realised he was kissing her eyelids and, through her tears, she kissed him back. She did not notice where Tengfei and Ai were, only that she and Peng drifted to his room. That they lay on the bed, embracing, for a long time. That they kissed slowly, deliberately; that their kissing and caressing began so imperceptibly at first; evolved into seduction.

Gui was supposed to meet Ju at the bar. He was annoyed because she had not showed up for their last practice session. In fact, she had been late for a few recently, always rushing in, red-faced from wherever she had been or whomever she had been with. He could guess what she was up to: seeing Peng. But her singing and playing, if anything, had improved. They practised some of the songs she had written and they were refined, Gui was impressed. They were both enjoying their new freedom, their ability to live their dream here in Jilin. So he turned a blind eye to Ju's relationship with the larger-than-life Peng. After all, he was spending time with the delightful Daiyu and Ju's absence gave him the opportunity for some privacy with her.

When Gui arrived at the *Inn of the Way of Happiness,* he heard Ju's voice as soon as he entered. He heard hands clapping and knew it was Peng. When he turned into the bar area, there they were, close together. Peng was crooning along with Ju, that sad song about Gui's sister's drowning. The hackles rose on the back of his neck to hear it come from Peng's lips. He was singing as if he knew her, as if she were some lost lover. Gui slammed his drum down so that it echoed, causing them to fall silent immediately.

"Are you alright, Gui?" Peng bellowed. He could not speak without shouting.

"Grieving for my sister," he muttered.

"I lost a sister to scarlet typhoid when I was young, I understand how long it can affect the heart."

Peng's sentimentality only enraged Gui more. He scowled.

"Well, I must go make arrangements for Dandong," Peng said to Ju. "But you look after yourself, Ju. I want to see you a star of Jilin when I return!"

Gui set up his drum and other instruments, tried not to notice as Ju and Peng hugged and kissed. When Peng had gone, Gui tried to launch into practising their first tune. The bar staff were arriving, but Ju insisted on probing.

"He came here to spend a last few minutes with me, for he leaves tonight on his tour."

"You don't believe all that, do you? That he would remember you when he comes back? If we're not playing the Hall of Celestial Sapphire or at the festivals at the Jilin Drum Tower, which we won't be, as it takes years to get in the good books of the organisers here, as Madame Fen told us that night she came in here to hear us, he won't be interested in you. He'll have moved on to the next hopeful."

"Peng cares about me."

"As someone does for a stray dog they have befriended awhile. People have told me what he is like."

"People? Daiyu, you mean? Who probably threw herself at him, as she does all men, and was disappointed as she is not musical. Peng is interested in me because we have a shared love of song."

Furious, Gui struck up their first tune, seeing the barman staring at them, waiting for them to start since the first customers had already arrived and were being poured their first drinks. He was too annoyed to counter Ju's argument with any more of his own, such as defending Daiyu – knowing that barb to be close to the truth – or trying to point out that it was Madame Fen's right-hand man, Gang, who had warned him about Peng. Of course, Gui could see for himself Peng was a blustering chancer; he

36

was frustrated Ju could not see it for herself, yet. And Gui was still young enough not to realise some things people just have to learn the hard way, through experience.

After their first set, as Gui swallowed a long glass of water, Ju hissed, "Why don't you come with me then to Dandong, see that it's true?"

"You're going there?"

"Why not? Our contract here ends in a couple of weeks. Peng will be there two nights, on tour, then back there in a few weeks' time. And Madame Fen says she has property there."

Madame Fen's man, Gang, happened to be nursing a beer almost beside him. Gui seized his sleeve. "Gang. Is it true Madame Fen has business premises in Dandong?"

Gang pursed his lips. "Dandong. Yes. A little place there, too. She used to have premises in Canton, but the protection expenses were crippling."

Gui was shocked again. "Too tough even for you?"

Gang laughed. "I am a pussycat, not a tiger! Men here know not to mess with me. But there, there you play with panthers. Canton can make the hardest of men humble."

Gui turned to Ju as she gulped down her water, now. "Ju, we were allowed to come on this adventure because my father wanted to assuage my sorrow on losing Guan-yin. And your father was relieved you were coming because he thought it would not be long before we wed, returned, and the shame of the incident would be forgotten. But they did not understand that your ambition to be a musician is as great as mine. I know you will go to Dandong for the adventure and to spread your wings. But it is my duty to go along and protect you, even if you would rather have nothing to do with me."

Ju shrugged her shoulders. "Is Daiyu coming, too?"

Gui thought for a moment. He stared across the bar to where the waitress was chatting amiably with a couple of punters. He shook his head. "She must stay here. But there may be someone else …"

Ju smiled, laughed. And Gui laughed with her.

Chapter 6

Canton, Late Autumn 1776

"Last night in Canton, Nathan!" his mate and fellow midshipman Richard Hume teased. "Come ashore, man! You've been far too dutiful. Just because your old man is captain, it doesn't mean you have to be a stick-in-the-mud. All work and no play makes Jack a dull boy!"

"I've seen plenty of Canton's bustling streets by day."

"You need a little recreation, come sample a little native music, Mr Gray," Lieutenant Foster cajoled.

Nathan liked Josias Foster's quiet confidence and knowledgeability, his consummate seamanship. So he dressed in civvies and disembarked with this tall, blond, chisel-chinned fellow, the squat, stout Richard and Captain Joseph, the only other officer taking leave that evening.

Captain Joseph led the way from the rickshaws to a street on the outskirts of town. There was a wooden gate that led to a park, across which the smoke from domestic fires curled to the early evening sky. The street bustle was replaced by the clatter of meal preparations as mothers rounded up children to come in from the park for dinner. An old man was leaning on the rail of the bridge. Captain Joseph went over and spoke to him in his own language.

"What did he say?" Josias asked.

"I said it was a beautiful evening. He said he was enjoying this tranquillity for he will not have many more."

"That's terrible, to think that way!" Nathan blurted.

Josias moved ahead, saying, as he tapped Nathan on the shoulder, "Only honest, he's an old coffin dodger. Where are we going to eat?"

Captain Joseph pointed. "Hong Lane, of course."

There was a long, winding street at the far end of the park, obscured by trees. Two rows of the typical Chinese low structures faced one another. The street was relatively quiet as the shops were closing up for the evening. But halfway along an inn was beginning to get busy. Around it there was some of the bustle Canton was famous for: hawkers with poles of fur mittens, hats, leather belts, scarves, with ragged children trying to sell steaming *beche-de-mer* or other delicacies on trays, snake charmers cross-legged on street corners, jugglers, lads playing an impromptu dice game, for money of course, a duel of crickets in a purpose-built, mobile ring, which Josias lost a coin on, dogs barking at them, even a stray pig refusing to move aside for them.

"Hog Lane, more like!" Richard quipped.

Joseph led them in. On their way, Nathan noticed the name over the door, *Inn of a Thousand Faces*.

As they walked along the street to the inn, a wizened old woman stopped him in his tracks by calling, "Nathan-yel."

"How do you know me?"

She pointed to her forehead, between her eyebrows, "I see."

Josias sneered, "Away with you," and walked on, towards the inn. Joseph went with him, but Richard loitered with Nathan.

"Let me see ahead for you?"

"How much?"

She held up two fingers, so he dropped the coins into her lap. She produced a metal bowl of water as he crouched beside her on his hunkers. Richard stooped to see, also. The old woman put a finger in the water, then let a drop fall onto the surface so that ripples disturbed it, before the surface settled once more. She concentrated on the surface.

"The past comes. Boxes thrown off a ship; burning torches; a pretty girl. She is in your future, but faintly, fleetingly. You will lose a father, gain two. You will marry a petite, dark-haired woman. Very pretty. Your love life will tend to be stormy, many highs and lows, but the relationship is long. A fire – the rain alight! And I see a darkness – a dark room – much time in a room – illness perhaps? For I see a death, almost death, and rebirth. I see a fork in a road – you take both paths; but one is much longer than the other, leads to your true destiny."

Richard laughed. Nathan thanked her as they strode on.

"Do you believe that rot? She knows folk at the docks, knows who we foreigners are. You, the son of the trader who has been here before. Boston – the tea party – that's easy. As for the future stuff, all the women here are dark."

"I'm damned if I'll be marrying any coolie!" Nathan retorted.

When Nathan and Richard reached the inn, two musicians were strumming in the far corner as a few tables of customers sat eating. The Boston men were shown to their friends' table by the excited innkeeper. They ordered food; chicken, pak choi and rice. Beer was brought. A couple of young women in silk dresses had appeared and stood giggling together at the bar, occasionally glancing over at the foreigners.

"Those girls seem to be unchaperoned," Richard said to Nathan.

"Perhaps that's the point," Nathan's tone in reply was scathing.

Josias's eyes bulged.

Captain Joseph's lips pursed wryly. He beckoned over the innkeeper. The elderly man with a wisp of hair over his balding head scurried over to them, stooped. Captain Joseph asked something about *Madame Fen*. The reply included *Jilin* and *Dandong*, at which Joseph's eyebrows rose.

"Ah!" the innkeeper shrilled as a young man arrived, girl on his arm. He went over to the musicians, while the girl joined the others at the bar. "Peng! From Dandong," the innkeeper told Joseph, nodding, before returning to his other customers as more arrived.

Peng began to sing.

Joseph told his colleagues, "I knew the previous owner here, but now she has moved to Dandong as her daughter married a man there."

Josias winked at Nathan when they heard Joseph say he had known the previous owner, and Nathan knew why Josias was suspicious of this Madame Fen. His suspicions were realised when, after several *baijiu* each, and chittering merrily, with a larger crowd in the hostelry, the girls from the bar slipped over beside them.

"You Boston sailor?" one asked Nathan.

Blinking delightedly, he told her, "Nathan! Captain of the *Firepower*!" and he saluted her.

She saluted him back. Pointing to herself, she said, "Baozhai." Then, pointing at him, she tittered, "Young Captain! Young Captain Nathan!"

Nathan scowled. But she placed a hand on his cheek and brushed his lips with hers. His eyes boggled. He stared across at his Uncle Joseph. Joseph was already arm in arm with one of these ladies.

The singer saw that the girl who had walked in with him was sitting chatting close to Richard. When Peng finished his latest number, he let the musicians play an instrumental and slipped across. He stood at the table.

There ensued a heated exchange between Peng and the girl. The innkeeper came across. Before he made it to the table, Josias and Joseph had stood up, were facing down the singer. Peng raised a fist but his arm was seized, Joseph and Josias had soon escorted him out. The girls fled into the next doorway. The innkeeper stood at the entrance of his tavern and screamed abuse at Peng. Josias and Joseph glared sternly at him, puffing out their chests. Peng squealed abuse at them all, but wandered off in a temper.

The excitement over, Nathan noticed Captain Joseph paying the innkeeper for his hospitality. The girls were peeking out of the doorway of the next building still, one beckoning them with a crooked finger.

Nathan stared at the others. Without a word, Joseph and Josias went towards that doorway and went in. Richard and Nathan followed.

There was a dim-lit corridor. Richard whispered to Nathan, "Aren't these the sort our mothers warned us not to associate with?"

Nathan replied, "My mother never mentioned such things." He gripped Richard's arm, guided him towards the brothel. "Canton System!" he joked drunkenly.

Before he knew it, Nathan was in a room alone with the girl who had kissed him. The others had each evidently entered through other doors to other bedrooms. She placed her hands on his chest, closed her eyes and raised her lips to his again.

"I like you," she sighed.

"*Wo xihuan ni,*" Nathan murmured in the girl's ear.

Nathan raised his shaking hands to her shoulders, closed his eyes, and allowed his consciousness to swoon into the ecstasy of intimacy.

Chapter 7

Dandong, Jilin Province, China, Late Autumn 1776

Captain Adam Gray was standing with his hands crossed behind his back as Joseph and Nathan scampered across the gangplank. Captain Joseph smiled broadly, handing the paper chit to Adam and saluting.

"You got the chop, then?" His shoulders visibly relaxed.

"Are you coming with us, sir?" Joseph asked his old friend.

"Someone has to watch out for the *Firepower* here."

"It would be fine in young Foster's hands, sir."

Adam hesitated.

Nathan heard Joseph whisper to Adam, "Fen's not in Canton. She's got a place in Dandong, now."

"Then I'm definitely not going!" In a lower tone, "Is that why you're going?"

"Not at all. Better tea from that region. And we've got the chop to go!"

"You'll have that pair along, too," Adam groaned, nodding at the two Chinese officials who were hurrying across the gangplank with kitbags on their shoulders. "No, you go ahead. I will scout around these parts for other commodities that we can trade."

Joseph stared hard at Adam. "Don't get caught."

Adam nodded gravely. "Don't you take the boy near that bloody woman," Nathan heard him hiss at Joseph, who nodded gravely in return.

Adam Gray shook hands with Joseph and Nathan and bounced across the gangplank. The men lifted it and a few dock hands lifted the huge ropes so that *Firestorm* was no longer tied up alongside.

"We're off, just like that! Captain Joseph thundered to Nathan, as the Leading Hand of the Watch piped on his whistle and the men raced to unfurl the sails.

Nathan stood blinking in the afternoon sunlight, watching his father's shape diminish on the dockside, the harbour itself move away and grow indistinguishable as the coastline stretched out and sea lapped all around their fragile wooden world. "Into the unknown," he commented to Joseph.

Joseph nodded. "God, don't you love it so?"

Nathan said in such a low tone it was barely audible yet sounded all the more profound, "I feel as if I have known this place all my time, as if I were meant to be here."

"Sailing's in your blood, lad," the captain replied.

Staring across the empty ocean ahead, then across the junk- and ship-spotted Macao Roads between the *Firestorm* and the red- and green-coloured wedge of land, Nathan shook his head, "No, it's not the call of the sea I sense, but some strange affinity to this fascinating land. I feel in my gut - as if something's about to happen. Something big. Something ominous ..."

A hand clapped down on his shoulder. "Meeting another floozy in some dingy, dodgy night hostelry?" Josias Foster guffawed from behind him.

Nathan scowled abruptly, stormed away from him and Captain Joseph's mockery at his expense.

Their first few days in the less picturesque - to Nathan's mind - more industrial Dandong, were spent sussing out the best deal for tea. Joseph and Nathan found a trader who took them up country to see the plantation where the rows of bushes stood, the drying sheds, all larger and more efficient than Canton's smaller, family farm-orientated business. The economies of scale also meant that these traders were able to offer larger quantities at cheaper unit prices. But it was the taste of the product which impressed Nathan.

At one point he whispered to Joseph, "We can buy this for less, and it tastes better than anything we've had before, or I've known others to supply, so we can get a premium price for it."

Joseph was a sailor, not the businessman his father was, so he nodded, impressed by Nathan's acumen.

Nathan enjoyed the trips by coach or rickshaw through the vast open land here. He sensed fresh air, believed he could taste a tinge of excitement in the air in this green country. He had never actually felt at home at home, in his father's brownstone on the very edge of Boston, where town met open countryside. In China, the grass was denser, lusher; back in Massachusetts, it seemed coarser, the whole landscape seemed harsher to him. Nathan saw it as his father's place, not necessarily his own. And he had been reared by a stepmother, of course. She was always, *Mother*, for she was the only one he had known. He had been summoned to his father's study one evening when he was fifteen and been told his birth mother had died when he was two. He was dark because she had been Oriental. A youthful folly, Adam had told him, to marry *one of those people*, despite being stationed in the East, for which the Christian Esmerelda had forgiven him and had the charity to overlook when he proposed.

Like all women, Esmerelda Gray seemed a distant, moody, unpredictable creature. Nathan considered women as another species, there for beautification and passing entertainment. But he took to heart the Sunday sermons about them, for what he had witnessed of them confirmed that capriciousness. So he gave them a wide berth as often as possible.

His puritan Boston upbringing had not yet quite been conquered: Nathan had not yet acquired Josias Foster's or Joseph Hearty's amoral attitude towards the fairer sex, though the longer he was in China the more the ancient wisdom of the *Canton System* was beginning to appeal to him, at least philosophically, despite his better nature and conscious inhibitions. Did not society back home operate a similar system in all but name? Concubinage was merely more open and honest in this country, they did not have the influence of Old Europe Puritans to flavour public attitudes.

All the same, back in Dandong for their last evening before the dawn tide, when Richard and Joseph suggested a run ashore, Nathan initially appointed himself officer of the watch. He was reluctant to be seen to be too keen to succumb to the temptations ashore. He should be above the others, show leadership, in all ways. But Joseph reminded Nathan that it was his only chance to see this northern town and he should do so in order to better gauge the place as a trading station for future visits. So Nathan reluctantly let the Master assume responsibility for a few hours and went with his shipmates into this vast, warren-like network of streets as darkness descended.

Only a sliver of a new moon lit the sky as they walked the short distance to the rickshaw rank. Nathan was asking the lead coolie where the best restaurant was when he heard Joseph asking about a particular hostelry, heard the names *Gang* and *Madame Fen* mentioned and *House of Raptures*. Richard had already got into a rickshaw with Joseph, so Nathan beckoned forth a few of the men from the ship who were just approaching.

"One of you can share with me."

"An. You're light, it'll make an even load for the coolie, sir," the petty officer suggested.

Nathan nodded and the burly cook's mate piled in beside him. The other men followed in their own rickshaws.

"I have not been in a rickshaw. I once helped my uncle pull, when we visited in Dandong, here, before I joined my first ship."

"Really? Your English is improving remarkably, An, well done."

"Thanks you, sir."

"So, you know Dandong well?"

"A little. I had wanted to be in the theatre, but I was only ever in background parts. But that's okay. But then I got drunk in a tavern and found myself on a ship! Two years ago!"

"Don't you be running off on us, An. You're a bloody good cook and a fine man to have on a boarding or repelling party."

"But theatre is less dangerous, Mr Nathan, sir. There you might only break a leg."

"They have recommended some tavern called, called the House of Raptures. It sounds - regrettable."

"Oh, Madame Fen's place is fine! Yes, they smoke there a lot, but it is about raptures of taste! Tasty food! And raptures of music, sir. Now we are given some allowance, now we are rich sailors, we can afford to eat there, too!"

"Good for you, An!" Nathan chuckled, as their rickshaws arrived in a narrow, two-storey street full of curry smells, music from inside hostelries and the hubbub of conversation.

Nathan joined Richard and Joseph at a table to the side, a little away from the gang of their men, who were soon snacking and drinking beer and rice wine with gusto. An was right about it being an opium den – the air was thick with the aroma of weed, the eyes stung with the billows of smoke on the air. At crowded tables, huddled men of all ages stooped over their pipes, casually puffing, as the acts of musicians and dancers changed in sequence.

A young couple scurried on stage as Nathan and his friends were having their third course. More *baijiu* was brought as the musicians began to play a haunting melody. The girl began to sing. The hubbub in the tavern quietened down, all were mesmerised by her beautiful voice and the captivating intonations that suggested, even to the non-natives who did not know what the words meant, an aching sorrow. When her song tailed off into silence, the place roared and clapped heartily. Nathan could see the innkeeper scowling at the girl, though.

An was nearby. He was staring at the girl with the awe of worship in his eyes. He caught Nathan's glance as the applause died down.

"She's very captivating," Nathan said to An. "You are in love with her?"

"She is my friend, Ju!" he cried, drunkenly. "We grew up together, in my home town, Songhua. So far away, north of here. We dreamt of being singers when we were small. Now here she is, on stage! A star! I can't believe it!"

An rushed off to his shipmates, was handed another beer. Meanwhile, a chair was drawn up between Nathan and Joseph and the innkeeper sat down, talking with the captain, partly in Chinese, partly in English. Clearly they knew each other. Nathan took from their conversation that this grey-haired fellow was Gang. But Nathan's attention was drawn to An's reunion with Ju, a few tables away. He strained to observe them.

Ju and Gui finished their set and went to a table vacated by the next act, to sit with a glass of beer. An strode over to them.

It was Gui who recognised him first and stood and bowed, grinning. An bowed in response. The two young fellows chattered away merrily. Ju leapt to her feet and hugged An. She talked rapidly with him. They spoke in their native tongue, of course, so Nathan could not make it out. This was the moment he determined to learn the language as soon and as thoroughly as he could.

"Where have you come from?" Gui had asked An.

"I was here, working in the theatre backstage and getting some parts when I woke up one morning with what I thought was a hangover but it turned out to be sea-sickness!"

"You were press-ganged? How terrible!" a hand shot to Ju's mouth.

"Well, I was on one ship to the Sandwich Islands, then got taken on another across to California. We sailed round the Cape to the east coast, Florida, New York, on up to Boston. I did not want to go on to Europe so I got on the *Firestorm*, heading home again. We were in Canton, which is great! Have you sung there yet, Ju?"

"Not yet. It's on our list!" she told him.

Gui sniggered.

"What? You think we won't make it?"

"I have no idea how we will fare as musicians. I just want to enjoy the moment."

"You'd be happy busking in Madame Lihwa's old tavern back in Sonhua," Ju was disparaging.

Gui nodded. "I am happy to tour, even for ever, but in the end older musicians often settle down. That would be a sufficient outcome for me, too."

"So easy-going!" An replied.

"Have to be, in our game," Ju said with all the seriousness of a five year old.

An laughed from the pit of his stomach.

"Are you going to jump ship now you're home?" Ju asked eagerly.

An looked over his shoulder. He could see Midshipman Gray sipping his *baijiu* and watching them intently. "Maybe …"

"Who's the foreigner?" Gui asked.

"One of your Boston men?" Ju asked with a shine in her eye.

"He's okay. He's the boss's son. A bit … bossy. Like all ship's officers. But he can have his moments."

"Moments of kindness?" Ju asked.

"Yes," An sighed. "Are you singing again?"

"We are supposed to do another set, three more tunes," Gui said.

With that, the innkeeper Gang reached them. He leant over. "You're doing fine. Although the crowd liked your version of Peng's song, he is here tomorrow night, so don't be stealing his thunder. Or any more of his songs."

As Gang walked away, Ju stared after him in disbelief. "What?"

"Told you," Gui hissed. "Peng's been here ahead of us, you know that, on his tour. You sang him your songs. Now he's gone and stolen them, made them famous - as his.

Who'll believe you wrote them, when he's famous as a song writer?"

"I'm sure he'll attribute them to me ..."

Seeing Gui and An's steely stares, Ju burst into tears. "I'll kill him!"

An put an arm around her shoulders, held her to his chest. "There, now, dearest Ju, don't let it overcome you. What did he get? A couple of songs? A couple of kisses? Ju, you have so many, far better songs still inside you, and so much true love to give, that bastard will not see their light."

Gui looked on as their childhood friend with the lisp comforted Ju as he wished to be doing. An noticed Nathan Gray watching again, smiled, and nodded. The midshipman pretended not to notice, looked away. Before long, Ju had to go with Gui and perform their last set. She did so half-heartedly, for it was others' songs she was singing, not the ones which came from her own heart. After their set, An hugged her goodbye for now, bowed to Gui who returned the gesture, and he left with his shipmates for their wooden home in the harbour. Ju noticed the table of officers was empty. They had, it seemed, gone back, also.

But when she went outside, carrying her instrument, Gui struggling ahead with his, a hand tugged at the covered horn on her shoulder. She wrenched back on the leather strap until a finger was marked.

"Hey, easy, woman!"

Ju stood back, blinking, seeing it was that officer friend of An's.

"I am just trying to help," Nathan told her.

Joseph and Richard had swaggered out, looking for the nearest brothel, which was not difficult to find as so many doorways in the street led to such places. Nathan had paused in the doorway of their choice, then let the other two swoon into the arms of the heavily-perfumed girls who greeted them. But the one who had approached him had not appealed to him.

Gang was hovering, said, "I get you new girl, sir. Wait, wait."

Having time to consider his immortal soul, his semi-drunkenness, and his full stomach, Nathan turned and bolted. Only to find Gui struggling past him with his double drum. Nahan recognised Ju from the tavern as she approached in the starlight. Instinctively, he had reached out to help her as she struggled to haul her horn up the steep part of the dark street.

Now, as she trembled before him, he touched his chest. "Nathan," he burbled.

She frowned. "Ning?" she misheard him.

"Ning!" he patted his chest. "Ning!"

"Ningcompoop!" Richard hollered behind him. "She's not one. They're in here!"

Nathan's face contorted into abject disapproval at having been confronted in such a way in the public street, even if no one for a thousand miles could understand a word either of them were drunkenly uttering.

Nathan shoved Richard back up the street and propelled him in the door of the brothel. Richard continued in of his own accord, then. But Nathan gave the tentacle-like, waving arms of the new girl the slip, so that he was soon on Ju's heels again.

"Don't worry," he said in a low tone.

Sensing his lack of threat, Ju let him take the horn and carry it for her. When she reached their room, Gui's drum was already dumped in the corner. She could guess where he had gone, whose company he had sought out.

The Boston man had sat on the mattress on the floor. Ju lit her tea burner, began preparing the paraphernalia. Ning watched her silently, intently. Neither of them could think of a thing to try to say, or convey across the language barrier.

"Very good songs," he told her suddenly. "Yours?" he nodded, cupping a hand to his ear, then making a writing sign.

Ju nodded, smiling, almost blushing.

Ning nodded his head vigorously. "Excellent. Moving." He rubbed an eye with a fist, to sign they had moved him to tears.

Ju froze. She had not expected praise, was taken aback, moved herself to be appreciated, especially after having just been accused of stealing someone else's work when they were her own compositions.

Ju shuddered as Ning was suddenly on his feet, towering over her, a rough hand on her shoulder, the other pawing at her face. Then, she realised he was wiping a tear from her cheek with a finger, ever-so gently – for his praise had literally moved her to tears. Ju discovered herself burying herself against his chest. Ning held her a moment, unsure what to do.

Their embrace eased. Ju turned to prepare the tea. When she turned to offer a handleless cup to her guest, she found him sprawled back on the mattress, mouth open, eyes shut.

Nathan came to late in the morning. The room was light. He found himself on the mattress, boots standing beside the wall, jacket and breeches folded on top of them neatly. The girl was curled up beside him, fast asleep. Carefully, he raised the light cover, to see she was dressed in a plain nightdress. Her tanned, bare feet stuck out from beneath the white, angelic garment. She stirred. He quickly let the cover drift back down onto them both again. As she woke, he pretended he was still asleep.

The girl rose from the bed. He peeked through half-closed eyes to watch as she raised the dress over her head, stood bare and so ineffably adorable for a moment, then put on her day clothes. She went to the end of the room, took a pot from inside a small cupboard, squatted over it and pissed, then put a cloth over it and put it back in the locker. Ju washed her hands at a bowl, then began making tea again. Last night's had gone untouched.

Nathan pretended to stir and wake now. He sat up. He touched his vest, emitted a mock exclamation of shock that his jacket was off. Ju laughed. She handed him a cup of tea. He bowed, receiving it from her. Sipping it, it tasted so good. He instinctively made appreciative sounds.

He stood up, wheeked on his breeches. He stared out of the window. The countryside beyond the town looked radiant in the morning sunshine, despite the crisp chill in the autumn air. Finishing his cup of tea, Nathan buttoned his jacket.

"I am afraid, though I should like to spend more time in your delightful company, Ju, duty calls."

Ju cocked her head. "Meet again, Ning."

He nodded. "I should like to meet you again. But our ship sails this evening." He made a sign, his hand a ship on waves. "Canton."

Ju nodded. She pointed at her chest. "Canton."

Ning laughed. "See you in Canton, then, Ju. And by then I hope our friend An will have taught me good Chinese." He signed a mouth speaking and pointed at himself.

Ju smiled, unsure what he meant but sensing affinity with this tall, aloof foreigner. She bowed as he straightened from pulling his boots on. Ning bowed back, then pecked her on the cheek as he left.

Ning was scarcely in the street with his back to the building when Gui turned the corner behind him and slipped through the doorway. When he went into the room, Ju was cradling a cup of tea.

"The Boston man was here?" he gasped.

Defensively, she retorted, "He was drunk, I could not let him sleep in the gutter!"

Gui pulled a face. "He could have slept at the house down the street."

"Did you?" she hissed back.

As he walked away down the street, Nathan wondered about Ju. Was she trustworthy, or just another coolie floozy? The drum was there in the corner, the drummer's things were there. What was that arrangement? There were two bedrolls, two slim mattresses she had pushed together, he noticed. And yet, if the drummer fellow was her lover, where had he gone in such a hurry? These Chinese lived cheek-by-jowl, it was hard to tell what way things were. Then again, he reminded himself, so many of the masses back home in Boston lived in a similar way in tenements, were as through-other as be-damned. For all her being a coolie, God she was achingly beautiful. Not only that, but there was something different, something he could not describe or pin down about Ju: a deep resonance in her eyes that connected with his soul, that echoed of incarnations and experiences long intimated or imperceptibly anticipated.

As he walked away, Nathan did not see Gui behind him, slipping into the room. Nathan did, however, see Richard emerging from the house of ill-repute ahead of him.

"I thought I was going to be late back," Nathan said, slapping his shipmate on the shoulder.

"Aw, don't, Mr Gray. I ache. All over!"

"Did she bite you?" he laughed.

"Where did you get to? Which one did you end up with? Not the fat pig?"

Nathan frowned. Where's Captain Hearty?"

Richard gestured with his sore head back at the brothel house beside the House of Raptures.

"Are you going back to the ship?"

Richard nodded slowly. "The walk will do me good."

Nathan told him, "Well, you go on. I will make sure the captain is okay and return him safely."

"Oh, he's okay," Richard chirped as he walked on. "He's in his element."

Nathan browsed at the bakery shop next to the brothel for a moment, purchased a hot bread roll. It was sweet. They sold him a paper cup of tea also. To line his stomach.

He reluctantly went into the brothel. It looked just like all the other houses in the street. It was quiet at this time of morning, there were very few women bustling about and the men were all already away to their work. Nathan expected to see some burly men guarding the place. As it was morning, there was no one in the corridors. A semi-covered girl briefly appeared ahead, from a washroom perhaps, moved across the hall and into a room. She saw him but did not pause. Nathan strode down the corridor to the room at the end, just round the corner, which had a glass panel at the top half.

A middle-aged woman was sitting behind the desk, looking over accounts. She had on a stylish green dress, pearl jewellery. She looked up, stared at him when he entered, closed the door behind him and removed his bicorn hat.

"I am from the trader *Firestorm*. My compatriot Joseph is here, I believe," he said loudly. "Do you understand me? I wish to find my friend and take him back to the ship."

He was surprised when the Eurasian woman said, in perfect Bostonian, "What is your name? I am Fen. This is my house. Your friend Joseph is here. He is fine. He is resting. He will be along shortly. Sit down, young man."

Nathan sat on the wooden chair before her. Unlike many Chinese rooms, here it was not the custom to sit on the floor. The European influence was evident. "I am Midshipman Gray. We sail soon."

As Nathan looked around the room, noticing the large paintings of Boston, New York and Dandong itself, Madame Fen was staring at him in amazement.

"The resemblance … You are Adam Gray's son?" she gasped.

"I am. My father is a respected trader in these parts. Canton, mostly."

"Well, respected by some, perhaps," she quipped.

A door opened behind her and Joseph strolled out, hat in hand, uniformed and ready for action once more. He leant over, kissed Fen on the lips passionately and moved towards the door.

"I couldn't help overhearing that young Nathan was here," he sucked in the words, rushing to leave. "Sorry, Fen, but we do have to sail."

"Typical sailors!" she called after them, not even getting up from her accounts as Nathan rose to his feet, bowed to her and followed the captain out.

"Come back soon!" they heard her call.

Joseph replied over his shoulder from along the dark corridor, "We will!"

When they were down the street and found a rickshaw, Nathan told the captain, "I feel uncomfortable that that woman knows my father."

Joseph chuckled. "He would, too. Especially knowing of your encounter."

Nathan pouted like a thwarted child. "I suppose he is only human. But I must say, though I did succumb drunkenly in Canton once to the charms of one of those creatures, and so can understand the weakness of ... moral rectitude, at the same time the ...sharing of them, the inevitable sharing of them, disturbs me greatly."

"Women must *share* men, too? Anyway, your father hasn't bothered with that woman for a long time. He was young. It was before he married Esmerelda Mulvenna."

"I don't wish to know whether my father has offended against mother or not. I would prefer no details, thank you, on that score. However, it is a relief to know it was in the past. Having made a foolish mistake in my own youth, now. Much to my regret."

"I'm not of the same mind-set as our fellow Bostonians," Joseph told him. "Though your father has graced me with the rank of captain, I am afraid, lad, I am a rough seaman at heart. I put on no airs and graces. I don't wish to be settled like respectable men. I love being an adventurer – and a rake. I like to drink, carouse and enjoy the company of frightfully unrespectable, loose ladies."

As they rocked in the rickshaw, Nathan let this confession sink in. "Well, you are an honest man, sir. I respect you for that. And the sea is in your veins through and through. I guess it is my destiny to be a trader as well as sailor and so I feel the burden of responsibility, the duty of providing a respectable role model to the men ..."

Joseph snorted dismissively. "Possibly. I would just say this, young man, and take it or leave it as you choose, but I do not swallow the lines we're fed, that enjoying life's

60

bounty is always to be forbidden. Or something shameful. All things in moderation, of course, but I think God made us to enjoy beer, spirits, opium, women, food, money."

Nathan was silent for a moment. He watched the lush countryside in the distance flit by; the verdant woods, the rows of tea stripped tea bushes marching to the horizon.

"At the risk of despoiling any sacred truths, I think we are the way God made us, and life's pleasures are there for being enjoyed, not denied."

Nathan told him, "From what little I have travelled so far, already I can see how difficult life is for so, so many. Why it is only to be expected they might grab what fleeting moments of pleasure they can, while they can. The pursuit of happiness …"

Joseph nodded. "But I risk hurting you …" he began, patting Nathan's knee. "By telling you, without wishing to hurt you or damage your inner self …" Nathan stared perplexed at him. "That woman, Fen, is your birth mother."

"My birth mother died."

Joseph shook his head. "She was left behind. They were married. Your father married your stepmother when he was more than seven years separated. So that is legal. And for all we knew at the time, she could have been dead. He was going to set up home here. But she went off the rails. Could not settle to his Western ways. Not so much because of her nationality, but simply she is one of life's free spirits. Not to be tamed. He appeared with the infant you on the gangplank as we were leaving. He didn't return himself for ten years, and even then was careful not to cross her path if he went ashore in Canton, he preferred to stick to Macao.

"We see how she kept herself. Resourcefully, as many must. Far more so than most – she is to be admired for not having sold herself short, but for having profited so profoundly in using the gift of her own half-caste looks so sought after by so many from both persuasions, in order to further herself. And then, in reaching maturity, rather than descending into destitution, she became the controller of others' destinies. She is a protectress to vulnerable and often naïve females while at the same time being to an extent a parasitical agent."

"How noble!" Nathan scoffed.

"I expect anger will come, and you will blame me."

"I won't mention this to my father. Unless he does so. Why bother? He knows she is here. As we left the ship ..."

"I had said there was talk of this Madame Fen here, in Dandong, for we knew she had absented herself from Canton. We heard rumours these past few years that she was around. She had been in Canton again, though he did not know it. I found her there."

"And struck up a friendship."

Joseph shrugged his shoulders. "I don't pretend to be some moral icon. She is long free of him. We are both free agents."

As the rickshaw reached the docks and the squawks of seagulls circled their heads, Nathan told his father's oldest, closest friend, "As they say, none of us are saints. If we were, what need would there be of preachers or prophets?"

Joseph tapped the back of his hand as Nathan stood to get out of the rickshaw. "I don't mean to upset him, or you, or anyone."

"I'm not bothered. And I wouldn't think he is, either," he replied grimly, tapping on his hat and bouncing across the gangplank to the sound of the bosun's whistle.

Chapter 8

South China Sea, Late Autumn 1776

Nathan Gray staggered with the ship's roll to the galley, cup in one fist. An was there, with Li, the cook. Li saw him enter and without a word being spoken between them, he took the cup and ladled a top-up from the tap-less, copper urn and returned it to him.

"Sir."

"Thank you, Li." Nathan sipped refreshing brew. "Say, An, you came back with us after all."

The big fellow scrunched up his face, querying his meaning.

Realising he had overstepped a mark, Nathan tried to make light of it. He whispered, "I thought you might prefer to be an actor in the theatre."

An raised an eyebrow, gave his head a non-committal shake. "We all dream."

Nathan nodded. "Yes. Some things are impractical."

Li had heard them anyway. "If An jumped ship, sir, he'd be rounded up in no time. Well, if he tried to hide out in any port. He'd have to disappear into a country town. And sure what use is that to a performer."

Nathan laughed with them. "You're very wise, An, to bide your time. I'm sure if you keep up your sterling work, before long you will gain your release and perhaps in the meantime have saved up enough to help you get a start in your chosen profession."

"Really?"

"If he saves, instead of drinking it all!" Li chortled.

The ship leapt like a salmon heading up a weir. Nathan caught the tea back in his cup like a circus juggler performing a trick. With his free hand, he steadied himself, saved himself from colliding with the corner of the work bench.

"Getting stormy," An commented.

Nathan downed the rest of his tea. "Better get back up to the bridge. See what's what," he muttered, handing the empty cup to An and hurrying for the ladder.

Once through the hatchway, Nathan balked at the blast of spray in his face. He staggered through the biting wind across to the wheel hand on watch.

"Where did that one come from?"

"Just blew up out of nowhere as you were down getting scran, sir."

"Are we battened down?"

"Aye, aye, sir."

"Have you sent word to the captain?"

"Just now, sir. Young Dando was up to get a lungful of air, I sent him with a report."

"Very good. We'll give it a little longer, see if we ride on without need of further action."

Captain Joseph appeared from the hatchway. He bounced across the bobbing deck towards them.

"How's things, Midshipman Gray?"

"All in order, sir."

"We've hardly got away from Dandong. Maybe by the time we get that far it will have calmed and we can get round by Macao Roads and up the Pearl River to Whampoa alright."

The ship listed badly to one side, before leaping back under the force of the gales that were swirling around them.

"We'd be safer riding it out first, wouldn't we, before going too close in to shore?"

"We need to see the coastline, know where we are," Joseph Hearty replied, peering through the spray and mist to see if he could spot landmarks on the shore on the horizon. "I think that's Fuzhou."

A violent blast sent all three of them reeling. The wheel spun. The seaman hurried back to it and tied it. The Captain was beside Nathan when the ship rolled again under the next blast.

There was a tremendous crash. They had not even heard the splitting of the timbers above as the top yard was snapped in half like a pencil and came vertically down. It pierced the deck, splintering its way through to the cargo hold. As the ship tilted again, a wave of ocean slapped into the hold.

Joseph and Nathan screamed at the seaman to come grab tarpaulin, patch the hole. Men came running from below to help, for they had heard and witnessed the penetration of their citadel. The gusts had eased for long enough that they got the patch roped before another deluge washed over the deck.

Captain Joseph staggered through the spray to inspect their efforts. He called back to Nathan, who was clinging on to rigging, "She's held, thank God."

A huge wall of sea swept across the deck. Nathan gripped the rigging for dear life. When the rollick of the vessel and the blinding whoosh of water had subsided, men were hollering.

"Men overboard!"

Nathan edged his way to the rail, peered out to see if he could spot their shipmates in the dark, billowing mountains of sea. Everyone was shaking their heads.

The hand of the watch stared at Nathan, "What'll we do now, sir?"

"Batten down!" he cried.

The men returned below deck, leaving just Nathan and the wheel hand clinging on to rigging.

Josias appeared at Nathan's shoulder. "The captain and William Barnes are lost?" he gasped, as the bitter wind attacked his face.

Nathan nodded. "You're first mate, I guess you're captain now."

Josias replied, "You're the boss's son, sir."

Nathan replied, "That's not a rank, Lieutenant. *Captain*."

Josias nodded. "If you're sure. Well, okay the, *Lieutenant* Gray. I guess you're first mate, now!"

Nathan's expression conveyed his shock at sudden elevation, also.

"What next?" Josias asked aloud.

"It's dying down already. Sit it out for a little longer. Get *Firestorm* into Fuzhou as Captain Hearty suggested. Assess the damage."

Josias nodded. "Make it so, Lieutenant."

"Aye, aye, sir," Nathan chopped back.

Chapter 9

Dandong, Late Autumn 1776

"Sir, you're some blagger!" Josias praised Nathan.

Ever since they lost Captain Joseph, Josias had treated Nathan with more deference. Nathan realised this was because everyone on the ship thought once they were back in Canton, with Hearty gone and Nathan having had a much sea experience now as he had, inevitably his father would make him captain. At least Josias was getting the chance to command, so that when another ship came up, or a voyage which neither Adam nor Nathan were to go on themselves, he stood in line to command again in his own right.

Josias worked professionally with Nathan. Nathan was glad, also, that Richard had taken the turnaround with good grace and had not taken umbrage against either of them that he was leapfrogged. He made the point, one day they were alone on deck discussing the latest sextant readings, of saying to him, "Midshipman Hume, you've the makings of a fine lieutenant!" just to let him know that, before long, he too would be in line for promotion.

Josias' praise this morning came as they left Fuzhou chop house with the requisite chit and customs official on board to allow them to return to Dandong for a replacement cargo of tea. The previous officials' verification of and terror at the storm that had claimed the captain's life and destroyed the cargo had swung it for him. The previous official had run a mile rather than risk another voyage on this, in his view, cursed vessel. It was gaining permission to return to Dandong on limited funds and owing the repair yard so much that was Nathan's coup. The fact that he had An and Li tutoring him for hours on end every day in the local lingo had helped Nathan – and his Chinese persona, Ning – to win over the chief official in the chop house. That and Ning's burning stares, in flirty reciprocation of the customs master's evidently illicit observations of the white Boston boy.

The saltwater had ruined their hold of tea. The lot had had to be dumped. Nathan was advised there would still be a holdful left in Dandong. And although it might be a lower quality, it could also be at a lower price.

"What are we going to pay the Fuzhou men with?" Richard had asked quietly, out of earshot of the customs official, one evening as they stood on the deck at sundowners, with Dandong on the horizon, supping their ration of rum.

"The Lord will provide," Nathan replied.

"I didn't know you were a religious man, sir."

"I'm not sure that I am, Richard! Are you looking forward to an unexpected return to Dandong?"

Richard nodded. "I liked this port. I liked the House of Raptures. The music is exquisite. Also, the *baijiu*."

"And the ladies?"

Richard responded, "Well, that goes without saying. But you disappeared on your run ashore. Where did you end up, or dare I not ask? Since you flutter your eyelids at customs masters for favours ..."

"How dare you!" Nathan snapped.

"Sorry! Sorry, sir! A joke. I meant no offence! Sailors are used to - indiscretions. Don't mind if - don't care ..."

Nathan leant his face into Richard's face. "I'm not being defensive. I fluttered my eyelashes at that customs master because I saw he was lusting over me and it helped us get the chop back to Dandong. But I'd not do that. I know some men, long at sea ... what they do. But I spent that night in Dandong with a woman."

Richard shrugged his shoulders.

"I want this kept quiet not because I want the men to think I am respectable, though I should like their respect. It is because, Richard, I think she is special. But," he sighed, "she is a coolie. Will I ever see her again? Am I a fool to fall for a coolie girl when she might be just another slut?"

Richard stared into Nathan's wide eyes as he backed off. "It's only natural to feel attachment to a woman. Sometimes we aren't sure if she's the right woman. But, well, some men, many men, like me, I venture to confess, are less virtuous than most women. There's no greater slut in Canton than me! I must confess that weakness of mine. Well, perhaps we return to Dandong for a reason. Not just to test our mettle as seamen and traders and adventurers, but in other ways? I'm not particularly religious myself, sir, but, despite all my sinning, in so many various ways, I have a sense of underlying spiritual significance to our lives that sometimes leaves me... breathless."

"My God, Mr Hume, we are such philosophers tonight. We've been too long at sea. We need a run ashore to blow the cobwebs from our skulls!"

"I'll drink to that, sir!"

Nathan, Josias and Richard took rickshaws to the House of Raptures. As last time, some of the men were out for the night and were also lined up at the rank. Nathan signalled for An to share a ride with him, just like last time.

"Deja-vu!" An quipped as they climbed into the rocking, creaking buggy.

"Is your friend still in Dandong?"

"As far as I know, sir. I hope I get to see her tonight. This morning, a delivery man that brought supplies told me Gui and Ju were still playing there a couple of weeks ago. They had hoped to tour, but didn't get anywhere yet. They have gigged at a couple of other inns around Dandong, but not got to Canton yet."

Nathan could not suppress a smile. "Perhaps we will have the pleasure of hearing her sing once more. Do give her my regards. She helped me out last time we were here."

"Oh?" An's tone was one of concern. Concern that a man of Mr Gray's standing might get involved with his friend, for such an entanglement, An was wise enough to know, despite his limitations, could spell danger for a woman of a lower rank in society such as Ju.

Nathan waved a hand. He was economical with the truth. "I was a bit tipsy. She saved me from falling in the gutter outside the inn."

An smiled and nodded, relieved. When they got to the tavern, An scurried in with his shipmates. They were soon chatting and jostling in a corner near the bar counter and small stage area.

Nathan joined the other officers at a table for dinner. Josias, as captain, ordered a bottle of claret. Over dinner, Josias asked Nathan about arrangements for going up country the next day, to order another load of tea.

"Good news. At the chop house this afternoon, the master told me there is a shipload of tea of a similar quality to what we had, in a warehouse at the dock. I've arranged to see the merchant at eleven. If we buy and get loaded up we could make the dawn tide."

"What about the cost? We're out of pocket after losing our cargo and there is insurance but it will be some time before payment."

"The chop master said the merchant has traded with my father in the past and will give us some leeway."

"The Lord works in mysterious ways," Richard commented.

"We're in luck," Josias added.

Nathan nodded.

The first musicians had finished their set and were packing up. Nathan noticed Gui and Ju coming on stage. Ju was approached by a heavyset fellow from the bar. They bowed to each other. All three were chatting. Nathan's jaw tightened. He tried to concentrate on eating, not be noticed watching her. He could not help himself.

"The next act," Richard commented, even giving Nathan a wink when he was sure Josias did not notice.

"They seem very pally," he replied caustically.

When the officers had finished their meal, they moved to seats by the wall. Gui and Ju had a longer set this time round. They were still playing as An bounded over, red-faced. He slumped down beside Nathan.

"When Ju and Gui finish, I will go talk with them!"

"They're still here, then. Who's the burly bloke?"

"Ah! I don't know him, but he's Peng. He's famous round these parts. He's just got in from Canton. He was touring. His songs are famous, very popular."

The duo completed their last song and bowed to the audience. They gathered up their instruments and left the stage area. As Peng's backing group began setting up, Ju saw An and hurried over to him. Her smile froze when she saw who was sitting beside him, with the tall, heavy cook's mate slumped uncomfortably against Nathan's shoulder. Nathan nodded to her.

In Chinese he told her, "Your songs are lovely as ever."

Ju chirped, "Thank you, Ning. But why are you all here?"

"We were nearly shipwrecked. We lost our cargo. We came back to get more tea," An told her in a slurred narrative.

Ju looked from An to Nathan. "Shipwrecked?"

"A storm. Some superficial damage. But the hold got soaked, the cargo was ruined. So, here we are."

"Well, I am glad to see you again, despite your trouble."

"And I you."

"And I you!" An roared, hugging Ju. "Where is Gui?"

"Oh, nosing round Peng, that swine who stole my songs!"

"He what?" An hissed.

"He came up to me just before we went on, for he didn't think he would ever see me successful, and apologised for the *misunderstanding* that others had thought the songs his, his versions of my originals. Pah! He doesn't care. He is famous and uses others' work to further himself. Thief! But, we must not annoy the likes of him, for he could destroy our chances."

An nodded. "Such is the world."

"Your right to your work should be protected," Nathan stuttered in faltering Chinese.

Ju smiled unconvinced. "That would be welcome. But how?"

"Do you get to sing again tonight?" An asked.

"No. Peng steals the show. As always."

"Well, said An, getting up, "I am already drunk. So, before I make a complete ass of myself, goodnight dear Ju. I hope to see you … in the morning," he began to whisper, realising the officers were sitting before him. "I might have to run ashore to collect some last supplies."

Nathan turned quickly to her as An walked away. "Perhaps a little air?"

They got up and discreetly walked away from where Richard and Josias were engrossed in a conversation about some nautical matter. They did not notice them depart together.

As they reached the street and began walking up the hill, Nathan asked, "No tour yet? No arrangements for Canton?"

"Not yet," she sighed. "Do you go to Canton after Dandong?"

"We might stop off in Fuzhou for a few days. A wee plan I am hatching."

"A life of adventure. And danger."

Nathan shook his head. "Calculated risk-taking, maybe. Besides, a ship is safe in a harbour, but that is not what they are built for. Ju, do you know Madame Fen?"

"Why yes. We met her when she stayed a few days in Jilin. Then, here, she has been in with her henchman Gang. She is very kind to young women like myself."

"Trying to recruit you?"

"Oh, no!" Ju laughed. "Well, maybe if I wanted to be recruited … Anyway, she is not just a business woman. She is a kind person."

"Do you think you could arrange for me to meet her? Secretly? Well, no, I mean, on the quiet. I mean …"

"Have you got a thing for older women?" Ju turned to tease him. She held his shoulder as she laughed in his face good-naturedly.

"No!" he blushed. There was the briefest of moment's pause and then Nathan placed his hand on Ju's arm, kissed her on the mouth. "You interest me."

Ju laughed again. "Interest!? Last of the romantics!" she teased. She skipped the last few yards up the street, in through the door to her quiet apartment building.

They entered the room. Ju lit a lamp. Nathan sat cross-legged on the mattress. "Is Gui your brother?"

"A friend. Chaperone. I suppose my parents think he is my boyfriend. His sister died, I told you."

Nathan nodded. Ju sat next to him, stared intently into his eyes. "I ... I am unaccustomed ... to ... feeling ..."

"Me, too. You are so lovely." He kissed her again. Her soft warm hand held his cheek as their mouths moved passionately in harmony.

They were dozing in each other's arms, beneath the sheets, on the mattresses so low to the ground, when the door clattered open and Gui clumped the instruments onto the floor. He did not speak but would have seen from the candlelight the seaman's clothes, the shape in the bed, despite the shell of darkness in that dingy, indecorous room with its faint musty aroma. He dumped the things and swiftly departed. Ju shifted, let her fingers caress Ning's buttocks again, and revived his ardour. They kissed more.

Ju's lips tugged from his. He opened his eyes to see what was up with her. "I'm on fire!" she whispered excitedly.

Ju swept the cover from them with an arm. Ning stared at her in puzzlement. Smiling, she turned, so that she was on her knees and elbows on the mattress, back arched, bare ass raised.

Over her shoulder she demanded, "Love me. Hard."

Nathan buried his face, made her moan. When Ju's shuddering had eased, he rubbed his palms over the two taut buttocks, seized hipbones with cupped hands, eased forward and fulfilled her wishes more and then his own.

They kissed and made love again, until they slumped, blissfully exhausted, fell asleep, spooning.

Nathan adjusted his jacket and lifted his bicorn hat. As Ju stood before him, he realised she must wonder when they might meet again. But he had other things on his mind. "May I ask when it might be possible to go see Madame Fen?"

"She rises early, I know. I have met her buying breakfast buns and rolls at the stall. We shall walk down to the bakery and if she isn't there, we can proceed to the House."

So they set off side by side. Ju was no Boston young lady, yet within he felt over-brimming with pride that this beautiful girl in the red silk dress patterned with swirling flowers and birds pecking nectar from pistils was with him. How he loved her bare, slim arms. How he loved that delicate, pale skin of her neck.

They got hot buns at the bakery, went on to the dwelling beside the House of Raptures. Gang was standing at the doorway this morning, smoking a pipe. Knowing their time alone was at an end, Ju turned to face Ning before they approached the servant.

She stared into his eyes with fervid dark pools of longing. "We do not know each other long, or much, but … I love you." Those last few words came out in an almost apologetic tone.

"I know exactly what you mean. I love you, Ju."

There was a flicker of a smile on her lips. He knew she shared his feeling: that she possessed this sense of shared life, being, too.

They said good morning to Gang, inquired after Madame Fen. Gang took them along the corridor to her office. She was finishing breakfast. Fen offered them tea.

"I'm here to discuss business," Nathan told them.

Fen said to Ju, "You can have your friend's undivided attention shortly. For now, I must let him speak in confidence."

Ju left the room without a word. She went to the doorway, stood sharing the pipe with Gang.

Nathan said to Fen in his recently acquired Chinese, "We were in a storm, off the coast at Fuzhou. Joseph Hearty was lost overboard."

A hand rose to Fen's mouth.

"Sorry to bear bad news."

"It's a shock, that's all. He was a good man."

Once the respects were paid in full to Hearty, Nathan said to the brothel madame, "I know who you are. He told me before he died."

"Who am I?"

"My birth mother."

Fen stared at him. Behind her, a clock ticked. "That is true."

"That is mainly why I am here. That is, I hope that that being the case, you might help me in my hour of need. I don't know who else to turn to."

"There are plenty of shroffs. It is their business to lend money. Why should I help you? You may have sprung from my womb, but you went with your father to the Americas when you were toddling. I don't know you. Why should I help you?"

"Because I am your son. Who was taken from you, I did not know it was the case. And I have no one else to help me escape ruin. The shroffs would rip me apart like sharks on a wounded porpoise."

"Helping you would be helping him. Why should I help that blackguard of a father of yours?"

"I am not my father. What benefits him only benefits him in the present. It assists me in the present and future."

"Why help you? You think you can just walk in after all these years, think I might actually *care*?"

"No. That is why it is a business arrangement. I offer you a ten percent cut."

"What's the deal?"

"I will get insurance to cover the lost cargo. My shipmates think the merchant will give me credit in lieu of the insurance on the loss. He won't. I need to pay him. But, I can get the next load for less as it is the end of season, remaindered after a dealer died suddenly. So our profit margin will be greater. So I can afford to offer you a cut."

"Fifteen percent."

"Twelve and a half."

Fen snorted. "You have my blood in you, after all."

She spat on her hand and held it out. Nathan spat in his palm and they shook.

"Just one thing," she insisted. "Don't tell your father."

The men worked hard loading the ship. Nathan hollered at the halfway stage, just when they were flagging, "You're doing great, men. Extra rum rations for three days if you keep this up!" It worked.

As the warehouse on the dockside was almost empty and the customs official, who was joining them on their journey back to Canton, had gone aboard to rest in his bunk, Nathan pointed out some sealed wooden boxes to

Simeon. He said he did not know what they were. He and Nathan prised at the lid of one with a crowbar. Peering inside, interesting contents could be seen. One red silk dress was visible at the top of the pile in the case that reminded Nathan of Ju: her jet black hair tied up on her head, her ebony eyes shining at him with promise and contentment. Nathan tapped the lid back down securely.

When the warehouseman returned, Nathan used his new language to ask whose they were.

"The dead dealer. They should have been taken away by the lawyer administering the estate."

"Are they junk, then?" Nathan asked.

The warehouseman nodded. "Cluttering up my warehouse."

"We'll take them away for you, dump them at sea, if you want."

He was very grateful. Nathan gave the word quietly to Simeon and the men to stow the tea-chests on board carefully, not burst any of them. Not mention them to the Hong merchant who was with them, either. As they left the warehouse an empty shell for the foreman to clean up, with a contented expression on his face, Nathan glanced up the road from town. He half-hoped to see Ju come wandering down from the cramped streets, red dress shimmering in the afternoon sunlight, pastel parasol on her shoulders, that natural, relaxed, endearing smile of hers evident. But she was not there to see them off, even if a couple of the men's tarts did show up on the dockside to wave them off with blown kisses, whoops and even a couple of tears.

After dinner that evening, Josias asked Nathan, "Did someone say you brought an extra thirty boxes aboard?"

Nathan whispered, "When we stop in Fuzhou to pay the merchants there, the first night, let's treat our Hong merchant friend to a night on the town. While he's recovering the next morning, we can slip them ashore."

Josias soon realised the reason why. The plan went smoothly. While the Hong merchant was lying in his bunk clutching head and stomach, Nathan called on a haberdasher. The boxes were brought. One was cracked open. He ran the silk dresses through his fingers. The finest cloth. Top price. No middle man's cut for the chop house appointed Hong merchant, either.

And so Nathan had all he needed to despatch Li and An by road to Dandong, with Fen's investment returned, plus her profit. An extra windfall, which still left the insurance money to claim. The damage to *Firestorm* was more than covered. Nathan glowed with inner pride.

When Li and An had safely delivered their consignment to Madame Fen, she shook her head in amazement. "That's the swiftest profit I've ever made. Well ..." she considered one encounter with a particularly wealthy Canton businessman that had been a windfall for a lost weekend, but that was not quite the same thing, even if it had set her up as an organiser and manageress. "Please return my thanks to Mr Nathan Gray, and express an open invitation for him to dine with me the next time he is in Dandong."

"We are to meet the *Firestorm* in Canton directly," Li told her. "If you are there in the next month or so, before we sail, I'm sure Mr Gray will only be too happy to invite you to dine."

Fen smiled graciously, flattered. "I'm not sure if I will be in Canton over the next few weeks. But, perhaps. If I am, certainly I will make a point of it."

Before leaving on a coach they had hired the next morning, An and Li had an evening to rest and relaxation. Of course they went to their favourite haunt in Dandong, Madame Fen's House of Raptures.

Li met a fellow he had been chatting with the last evening they had been here. They shared puffs on an opium pipe.

Without his shipmates to get drunk with, the usually shy eunuch An snuck backstage to the rooms where the artistes waited. He gingerly knocked on a door, heard a female voice reply. In he swung.

"Ju!"

"An!"

"Li and I were sent back, on a secret mission!" he whispered.

They sat and conspired. An told her everything, though he was not supposed to. Ju was intrigued.

"Ning is a very resourceful man."

"Ning?"

"Well. I misheard what I was told his name was. It stuck between us, a kind of joke."

An nudged her. "A kind of private joke!?"

Ju tried to ignore the implication. "What about you, An? Have you found any happiness?" "You mean, a meaningful friendship?" He sighed. "Do I ever? You know what *people* are like," he confided. "Usually selfish. Not usually interested in the real me. For the real me is … clumsy, and daft, and a burden …"

"Don't hang your head, dear An. The real you is kind, helpful, trustworthy, cheering, and so sweet."

"Aw, my friend!" They hugged.

At that moment, Peng and Gui walked in.

"What is this!" Peng roared.

"An is my friend!"

"Out, you monster!" Peng grabbed at An's shirt, trying to haul him to his feet and propel him through the door.

An hauled back. He was about to swing a fist at the singer when Gui held him arm down.

"Easy, fellows! There's no need for this."

"I'll see you soon, Ju!" An said to her as he stormed away.

Gui went after him. "An! They're not an item. Not that I know of, anyway. He's just a bighead and a bully."

"Why put up with him? He stole her songs."

"We won't be here much longer."

"Come to Canton with us, Gui. There's room in the coach."

Gui thought for a moment. He smiled broadly. "I'll tell Ju."

When he did tell Ju, her face lit up too. "But we owe two month's rent, Gui."

"So?"

"We may need to come back. It's not right."

He nodded, face downcast.

"I might have a way ..."

Gui gave her a withering stare. "Don't ..."

"No, no. An honourable way."

And so, when there set was complete, though Madame Fen was not there tonight, Gang was. So Ju slipped onto a chair beside him. He told him her predicament, how she hoped Madame Fen might help in some way. He told her to come to see Madame Fen in the morning.

When Ju went at breakfast time, Madame Fen poured her a cup of tea. They sat in her office, making small-talk for a time.

"And also, there is a man on that ship of An's whom I … like."

Fen curled a lip. "To be young, and not disillusioned by love. But, really, my dear, a sailor! They're such rough, careless fellows."

"This one's an officer. Ning, well, Nay-than," she tried to pronounce the alien syllables deliberately.

"Nathaniel Gray!?"

"I was with him when he came to you, to speak with you, remember?"

"Oh, my dear Ju, age is such a curse that I would forget something so recent. Of course you were. I thought you were just showing him where I was …"

"Is Ning not to be trusted?"

"I was wary of him, Ju, to begin with. For years ago I knew his father and I was disappointed. On the contrary, however, Nathan so far has exceeded expectations."

Ju knitted her perfectly-lined eyebrows. "He is your lover?"

Fen laughed loudly, for a long time. "He will never be that! Don't worry on that score. My dear," she placed her hand on Ju's, "I do suspect you are in love with him."

She nodded and shook her head at the same time. Tears dripped into her teacup. "I ache inside. I know it's foolish. Why should I care about a … tall foreigner, a Boston man?"

"Love does not discriminate, my dear."

"I can't help it. I am indifferent, yet I care … I don't know …"

Fen nodded. "I once fell in love with a foreigner, a Boston man."

"Really!?"

"I was disappointed, Ju. But I believe you won't be. This Nathan has a finer pedigree. Well, at least in part. Fifty percent, to be exact. He is *my* son."

Ju stared, incredulous.

"His father married me. I was only your age. Of course, I was wilful, I admit. Had airs and graces, wanted to run an empire from a huge house. I was brash, bossy, over-confident. Still am, of course!" She sighed deeply.

"You have right to be. You have made so much of yourself."

"A concubine, a harlot, a madame is what I have made of myself."

"You're one of the wealthiest people in Dandong!"

Fen gave an embarrassed smile, shaking her head. "I am still a madame."

"And so? It is a business the same as any other, for those who want …"

Fen interrupted, anxious. "But this Ning of yours, this Nathan, he is not his father. And you are not me. So"

"Now I feel awful. Because I came here to ask a favour. And now you have told me all this, I feel I am imposing."

"Just ask, Ju. Tell me what it is."

"Their ship is on its way to Canton. The two sailors, including my friend An, have a coach to take them there. They have said Gui and I can go. If we went, we would be able to try to get work in new venues. But we owe rent here."

Madame Fen began writing furiously. "Here. This is a note to the proprietor of the Inn of a Thousand Faces. I know him well. I ask him to give you a trial. How much rent do you owe?"

"Two months. But …"

Fen took out some money. "Here is enough to cover that. And the same again to get you started in Canton."

"It is a loan. When my songs become famous, I will repay you, Madame Fen. I promise," Ju said with fierce pride.

Fen waved a hand, reached to sip more tea. "What is the point in having money if you cannot use it to do some good? Can't take it with you …" she mused.

Ju expressed her gratitude and surprise excessively. Fen held a finger to her lips. "Repay me with a hug!"

They embraced.

"Go, now, dear, and enjoy your adventure! Ah, to be young and fearless!"

Chapter 10

Canton, Early Winter 1776

An, Li, Gui and Ju reached Canton after the *Firestorm*. They had nearly three thousand kilometres to travel, it took them over three weeks by coach. The ship had nearly the same distance but, despite their stop in Fuzhou, they took only half that time. Plus the two men had travelled from Fuzhou to Dandong in the first place.

When the *Firestorm* reached Canton, Adam Gray had unanticipated news. The death of his friend of many years. The ruined cargo. The replacement cargo and the bonus deal with the silks. He was at once saddened by Joseph's death and privately elated by his son's cleverness and success.

They spent the last few weeks at Whampoa Island inspecting additional goods. Adam had purchased a load of chinaware to take to Boston. He was approached by a local trader, however, to take an uninventoried load up to a small harbour near Fuzhou. He discussed the venture with Nathan alone, over dinner at the Inn of a Thousand Faces.

"A load up the coast?"

"The *Firepower* could get a hold-full of tea in Dandong, surely?"

"There is more to be picked. The last picking of the season, in the southern regions around Dandong itself, yes. But I thought we agreed it would bring home chinaware?"

"There is a greater profit margin in the tea, if it is at the prices you have managed."

"True."

"And," Adam whispered, "The other venture would mean additional revenue. You realise, you'd have to get the chop house man drunk. The unloading would be at sea, to junks."

Nathan stared at the fellow at the next table, openly puffing on an opium pipe. Adam nodded.

"Risky."

Adam nodded again. "After all, we have time before the winter storms arrive. And your two men are not back yet."

"Pah! I wouldn't wait for them. I doubt if we'll ever see them again."

"You think they'll have absconded with the money for this trader in Dandong?"

"No. They wouldn't dare do that. That's why I chose them. Li might slink back. The other fellow, I think will disappear. But he won't steal. If he does come back, I may even offer him his release. He has foolish dreams of a career on stage."

It was then that Nathan noticed Gui talking with the innkeeper, over by the foot of the stage. There was Ju! Obviously giving the innkeeper a piece of her mind. He was having none of it. The act on stage finished and Gui got up, but alone.

"Excuse me, father," Nathan left the table, made his way through the busy crowd of customers to the bar and stage area. At last, he found her, huffing at a table, squeezed in between some burly men. Ju looked up to see

Ning staring down at her. He stared at the man next to her and the local fellow dutifully edged aside to let the Boston man sit beside her.

"Have you eaten?"

She shook her head. He called over a waiter and ordered food for her.

"I can't believe you're here, Ju!"

"An and Li gave Gui and me a lift in their coach. You paid my way here, Ning! But I am very grateful. Gui and I are going to take a chance on spreading our wings, getting a name for ourselves in new venues. Only ..."

"Are my men back in town?" Nathan interrupted her.

"Only this afternoon. We came here, got lodgings arranged, then straight round here to do some songs. And then the bloody innkeeper wouldn't let me on stage! He disapproves of women singing. It's okay for them to dance and serve men in other ways, but not to sing!"

"I'll have a word with him later, before I leave."

"It won't do any good. He has heard I sing Peng's songs. So he doesn't want to offend the great Peng by letting me perform here."

"The songs he stole from you?!" Nathan shook his head. "Don't worry. Look, just practise with Gui, other songs Peng doesn't know. When the innkeeper gets to know you a bit better and trust you, he'll let you sing."

"I suppose you're right, Ning." He noticed she was touching his arm.

"Meet me outside when you have finished your meal."

Nathan went back to his father's table. "Do you want Josias and me to take the *Firepower* north, then, since we dealt with the ones in Dandong and Fuzhou?"

Adam nodded. "At my age, it is nice to be able to just be stationed in one place for some time. I like to walk in the fresh air and see the countryside. Now you have learnt the ropes, Nathan, perhaps after we return home, I might not voyage any more. Manage things from the Boston end. Spend more time with your mother."

"Mother? Yes. How is she?"

"Some letters came last week. All's well with her." Adam smiled dreamily, thinking of Esmerelda at home.

"Now I have seen something of the world, sir, I am realising what a blessing a happy marriage can be."

Nathan yawned, deliberately. Adam caught the yawn.

"Perhaps I should return."

"Well ..."

"You're young. Your shipmates are here. Old Simeon and I will share a rickshaw to the ship. Enjoy yourself. You've been cooped up on the *Firestorm* for so long."

Nathan agreed. He watched as his father and the aged hand left. He saw Ju had finished her meal, was chatting merrily with one of the local fellows sitting beside her. A rage of jealousy flared through his system. Would she never come on? He caught her eye at last, jigged his head to one side to beckon her out.

As they met at the doorway, stepping out into the street together, she asked, "Won't you stay a little longer? Gui played so well. And that next fellow is an excellent singer. I could listen to him all night." Her eyes glazed over dreamily.

"It's late," Nathan commented, escorting her firmly, gripping her arm.

"An said he was sent on a mission to Madame Fen ..."

"What did he say?"

"Nothing. Don't be angry. He told me that and only that. What do I know of your business with her? Have you anything to tell me about it?"

"No! Nothing much. She helped me out, lent me money. I paid her back, with interest of course. But that is private."

"Of course. Well, at least you didn't owe her a huge slate from her establishment."

Nathan laughed. "Never! Are you jealous?" He tugged her close.

Ju merely tugged him closer, buried her face in his neck.

"I have missed you," he whispered.

"I've missed you, too, Ning."

"You're special."

"No I'm not!" she laughed.

They kissed, then made their way to her lodgings.

Nathan's ship had sailed that morning. Ju had not wanted to consort with Peng again, but he had shown up early in Canton. Here he was, strutting about like a peacock, making everyone laugh with his casual lines. Making everyone swoon with the power of his voice as he rehearsed.

Ju knew it was a mistake to let him squeeze her bottom when they were standing chatting. She was going to slap his cheek but the way he diverted attention from his liberties with the jokey stories he told Gui.

It was by Gang's face like thunder that she knew she was in trouble. He came over and spoke to Gui. He ignored her: she was a mere female to him, not an entertainer in her own right. She burned inside, knowing this Madame's lackey looked down his nose at her. But Ju held her tongue. She had done enough damage already by allowing him to think she was one of Peng's playthings.

If she had been, it was brief and – a mistake. She wanted to obliterate it from her mind. Hadn't he turned up in Canton with some new girl, as ever? Some discardable piece of fluff. Some poor girl like herself who thought he meant what he said when he said he'd help. He'd help himself, more like.

Ju asked Gang, "Are you in Canton for long?"

"A fleeting visit. On business. I must return first thing in the morning."

Damn! she thought. "Master Peng has notions above his station."

The master was on stage, crooning. One of the ones she had penned, but he had commandeered.

"He has written some fine songs. But this one, he is singing now, he *borrowed* from me. Not the other way round."

Gang frowned. "He's been singing this song for ages. You've only just arrived on the scene."

"Not that long …" she tried to protest. Ju realised it was no use and dropped her faltering campaign for justice. She was beginning to realise she might have to play dirty in this dog-eat-dog world in order to achieve her dreams.

"Have you known him long? Do you know him *well*?" Gang's tone pierced.

Ju stuttered, rather than admit any truths. "No … no … How is Madame Fen? I am most grateful to her! Gui and I are so lucky to be here. We truly appreciate this opportunity to learn our trade further, to develop, to fulfil the trust others have placed in us."

Gang was watching Gui, for he had been summoned by Peng to play and sing with him. "Gui is a good fellow."

"Yes," Ju acknowledged. "He is." Again, she bit her tongue, despite the rage within that the man should get praise, she, the female, be overlooked yet again. She realised, also, she would have to work twice, three times as hard just to get half the attention Gui would get. Ju knew she was the better singer and at least an equal musician, but no, she would always be playing second fiddle in this life, she could see.

Gang left. Peng had the innkeeper serve them all a delightful meal of plain home cooking, rice and steamed vegetables, a portion each of tender pork. All the musicians, singers, dancers and comedians enjoyed each other's company around the tables set together. Ju loved this part of this life. She felt she belonged here. Among themselves, they realised each others' talents and worth, even if once they met the outside society its tentacles of prejudice and favouritism slithered in.

When the evening came and they took their place on the stage, Ju tried a new song. Being nervous, it only half-worked. But she was glad she had tried it.

Their time was cut short when Peng appeared at the bar. Some of the crowd saw him and chanted for him. Before Gui and Ju could start their last tune, Peng bounded centre stage and began singing without backing. Gui obliged. Ju did not know this one and found herself edged off as Peng's band arrived. Gui bowed and left when the first song ended.

They had a beer each and stayed for the set. Peng moved seamlessly from one song to the next. Near the end, he launched into that new song she had first sung an hour or so before. He sang with greater confidence and conviction than she had. He had changed the lyrics to suit a male singer, and played fast and loose a little with the arrangement. It sounded much better this way, given that it was a male voice. All the same, it was a twist of what she had aimed at conveying. The crowd seemed not to recognise that she had just delivered a similar version. Her version had met with polite applause. Peng's version was greeted with roars, claps, cheers.

"He makes me cry," Ju heard one young woman tell another. Ju cringed inwardly.

"I'm tired," Gui said as Peng's set ended.

"Don't you want to stay and party with your mate Peng?"

"He's more your mate than mine."

As they went outside to go to their lodgings, Ju asked him, "How could he do that? He only heard it once tonight. He couldn't do that. No one could. Adapt it like that, so quickly. Gui … You have played with him before?! You gave him my song! This one we have been practising and refining for months, before I would dare to try it publicly. You would do that?"

"Ju. It's a song. A nice song. Not a special one. You do write really good ones. If he and I tried out a few songs that are … mediocre …"

"Don't you ever give anyone any of my songs again." She was beyond anger. But her tone was adamant. He knew not to mess with her work again.

"I'm sorry, Ju. I have offended you with my unthinking attitude. Your compositions are all special to you, of course. I hoped if he liked some, he would help us. By hearing our work from him, people will recognise our abilities."

"You know already that isn't true. You know already they just think they are his."

"I thought that wouldn't happen again."

"Well, it has. Thanks to you. More of my work, stolen."

"That's a bit harsh."

"It's true."

They walked on in silence a moment.

"You know, Ju, although he was not so kind to you up until now, he does really like you."

"Why would you think that?"

"Men don't often confess such inner feelings to others. But, I could detect in the way he talked about you. There is an underlying affection perceptible, he may not even be aware of himself."

Ju stared at Gui. "But isn't he - selfish?"

Gui nodded. "Isn't life difficult for people like him? Everyone wants a piece of them. Who can he trust? Girls flock to him because of his fame, not for himself. Apparent disinterest can be a shield."

Ju hesitated at the entrance to the lodgings.

"Go back if you like."

Ju hesitated still.

"It doesn't have to be serious. It doesn't have to mean anything. This sailor fellow. Where's he? Halfway to Fuzhou? Does he care to stop with you? A girl in every port? Which one of many are you?"

"Ning isn't like that."

"Isn't he? He's a man, isn't he? A Boston man, here for a short time, before returning to his fancy Boston friends, the ladies in their long white lacy dresses. Does he really care that much about a coolie? It's up to you. But it does no harm to be a friend with someone like Peng. You don't have to let him use you. Unless you want to. As long as you get what you want out of it. And, who knows, in time, it might just be the route to ..." Gui pointed up to the cloudless night sky.

Ju stared hard at Gui. Slowly, she turned and began walking back to the Inn of a Thousand Faces.

Chapter 11

Dandong, Early Winter 1776

The *Firepower* was a contrast to *Firestorm*. The ships were identical physically, but the atmosphere and character of the crew were perceptibly different. The men on this ship were more subdued, more mature. It was partly their being a little older, on average, there being less recently pressed men aboard, but perhaps also the fact that this was Captain Gray's vessel and he was the ultimate commander. Many of the men had sailed with him for many years, were loyal and obedient. There were certainly less spats among the men on this ship.

Nathan's plan, to render the Hong merchant, Mr Wu, drunk as they reached Fuzhou, then meet junks that would ferry the illicit opium cargo away, worked perfectly. They had a dark night and a calm sea, despite the time of year. Adam Gray had already despatched Richard by land to meet the recipients and complete the trade with them. He made his way with his native men to Dandong, to meet *Firepower* there.

If the customs man suspected anything, he turned a blind eye. Better to allow the Boston men some leeway, some chance of making a living, so they would continue the lucrative trade everyone benefitted from. The customs house itself brought in revenue for the Emperor, maintained the chop house men's careers, he would not rock the boat.

Firepower docked at Dandong in record time. Nathan and his father's first mate, Iain McKinley, journeyed up country with the Hong merchant. This time, they headed east instead of north. Nathan found a trader and a good deal. He arranged for a shipload of quality tea to be brought to the port. They returned to Dandong elated.

To celebrate, they headed for the House of Raptures. Nathan ordered Chinese wine, chicken, rice, bean shoots, bean curd, and a variety of delicious sauces. Madame Fen suddenly appeared at the fourth space. Tea was brought. She offered them some, which they all accepted.

She told Nathan and Iain, "You know, our Emperor Shennong was on expedition in the south of the country, about three thousand years ago. His men would boil water to purify it before drinking it. Often, they would not wait for it to cool, have it lukewarm. This day, some leaves from a bush blew on the wind into the pot. No one noticed. The Emperor drank the steeped juices, rather than waste the water. He was so surprised by the refreshing sweet-bitterness and reviving nature of the brew that he ordered leaves be picked and brought with them. And so the art of tea-making began. And China's love affair with *the sweetest dew of heaven*."

"And we are honoured that he did so, Madame Fen, for his discovery has led to our being here, in this beautiful country, among your fine people. We are blessed to be able to enjoy your wonderful tea and cultivated society."

Madame Fen smiled and bowed her head in gratitude. Iain winked at Nathan as they all sipped their tea, carried on making small talk.

"In Boston now, since our tea party a few years ago," Iain told her, "we have become coffee drinkers. But the commodity itself is desirable enough, if it comes limey tax-free."

"You dodge the colonial customs net? How gallant!"

"Not so glamorous, nor as difficult as it sounds. You just pick the place and time, avoid their patrols. They'll soon catch on that when we say we're independent, we mean it."

Despite the early hour, Madame Fen did not spend long with them. She soon excused herself.

Leaving, she said to Nathan, "Perhaps you will talk with me a moment before you leave? I will be in my quarters."

Nathan bowed as she left their table. Her back was scarcely turned and Iain was supressing laughter.

"Behave!" Nathan warned.

"She's gone!" he whispered, his eyes glinting with mischief so that the Mr Wu could not help himself but chortle also. "Gone to wait for you, you dog! A bit old, but have to keep the influential ones content, whatever you have to do!"

"She's not like that."

"She's a madame!"

"Not like that with me, I meant."

"Yet!" Iain continued to dig.

Nathan had to let it go. Besides, at that moment the comedian was booed off, to be replaced by the singer Peng. He had a raunchier show tonight, with three girls doing a risqué dance around him. Nathan scoured the room but Gui and Ju were nowhere to be seen.

When the other two had had enough of drink and song, they got up to go. Knowing they were moving next door, Nathan made his excuses.

"I may join you later. I must pay respects first."

Iain's face expanded like a balloon, but he did not get a chance to comment.

Nathan made his way out the back corridor. There was a doorway led from this house to the next. There was no one on guard. At the door to her apartment and office, however, Nathan heard voices. Fens and a voice he recognised as Gang's. He listened at the door a moment.

Gang was telling her how the girl Ju and the boy Gui had been performing in Canton. The girl was consorting with Peng, though he had only gigged two nights down there, then wound his way back here.

"He's just arranged a stint in Xi'an," Gang told her.

"Impressive. But Peng is using that girl Ju, as he uses everyone. Can't she see that?"

"She thinks he will help her to get famous."

"Bloody fool! Maybe he will. At what cost?"

"He seemed to be more than usually fond of her."

"Oh? That's not good. I thought she had more sense. I had hoped she wouldn't take a similar path to the one I did – compromising oneself in order to enrich oneself."

"Don't we all do that?" Gang responded.

"I thought she liked the Boston boy."

"I hear he got a good deal, as you asked."

"He doesn't need my help to seal a deal. But if my intervention helped

"Hard to say."

Nathan knocked the door. It opened. Gang bowed and departed. Nathan went on in.

Madame Fen was resting on an elaborate, baroque-style chaise longue. "Ning! Nathaniel!"

"Ning? How come you called me that?"

"It is how your name sounds to a Chinese ear."

Nathan was wondering now how well Fen knew Ju and what might be going on behind the scenes. "I came to say goodnight. You seemed tired, earlier."

She nodded. "I am unwell. Exhaustion pervades a lot, these days."

"Oh."

Staring at him earnestly, she said dismissively, "Acupuncture relieves it. In the longer term, I am destined for an early grave. But, if such is my destiny, what can one do."

Nathan moved forward, touched her arm. "I am sorry that that might be the case."

She tapped his arm. "You're a good boy. Now, sit down and tell me all about your latest time in Canton. Is your father well?"

Nathan sat to talk with her. He realised she was not the slightest interested in his father. "He was upset to learn of Joseph Hearty's shocking loss, of course. But he was pleased we had done so well in sourcing the upcountry tea. So, we returned for a second hold of it. It will command a premium back in Boston."

"You will sail soon? Such an adventure, here, for a young man like yourself."

"It will be pleasant to return to America. But I am already a convinced sailor. I intend letting my father know I wish to spend time at sea. Well, I feel I can make good for the company, and the family, based in this country."

"You like China?"

"I feel more at home here than in Boston."

Fen's eyes lit up. "You will keep me alive until you return, awaiting your ship on the horizon again."

"I didn't realise your ailment was that bad!"

She shook her head. "Perhaps not. Who knows. The fears of an old woman."

"Old!?"

She laughed. She used a land to gesticulate, using it as a ship on Imaginary Ocean. "Suddenly, I feel aged beyond my time. The scrapes I have been through. With business deals of my own. Officials to avoid, officials to navigate around, businessmen to assuage in order to get my own passage through the reefs of society."

Nathan nodded. "I can admire your ability to survive. I enjoy the cut and thrust of dealing."

"When you're winning, it's fun. But. It is getting late. You need a little comfort before you return to the ship. Go on through," she whispered, gesturing towards the business end of her establishment. "After so long at sea, you need some company."

He pulled a face, draining the tea cup which, inevitably, had been set before him on a side table.

"Or perhaps your heart is captivated by one in particular? One who embodies China for you?"

Nathan rose to his feet. He shrugged his shoulders, giving nothing away. "I am an explorer and adventurer for now."

He leant over, kissed her, departed.

As he was going through the door, Fen told him, "Don't make my mistake: don't think adventure and excitement are more glamorous than, well, ordinary life."

"My father's steadfastness, or as you might call it *dullness*, pervades my nature."

"Ah! There's a mote of risk and pleasure-seeking in there, too. And more than any body's fair share of wilfulness. All of which my blood has cursed you with. I just hope you can be happy where I could never be satisfied."

Chapter 12

Canton, Early Winter 1776

The *Firepower* returned to Canton's trading area with its cargo of the desirable commodity, tea. Nathan went with his father and the hoppo to their warehouse space in the factory on Whampoa Island and arranged for the loading of the other goods Adam had bought in Nathan's absence: chinaware, some bamboo furniture, some Buddhas and other *objets d'art*.

Adam said he was going back to the ship for a rest and light supper. The men were mostly off to a local bar, drinking. Josias and Richard were both on duty, one on watch, the other catching up on preparations for sailing soon.

Nathan took a long walk into town. The taverns were just opening up as he reached the entertainment area. He wandered into the Inn of a Thousand Faces. He ordered some food. Nathan saw An, alone, eating over at the far end of the room. He joined the seaman.

"No Li or other friends?"

"All gone drinking. If the tide is right we sail tomorrow, if we get the Grand Chop. So, I came to see my friends Ju and Gui before we go."

"You know, An, you don't have to come to Boston with us. You could stay here, see if you can get a place in a theatre troupe, helping out. Here, maybe?"

An stared in disbelief. "You'd release me?"

"We have enough men."

An though about the proposal while he ate. "I have little to get me started."

"You would be due your pay on release. After two years' service, quite a lump sum. I will sign the papers in the morning, if you wish. And Li -"

"He will stay aboard. He likes life at sea."

"What *will* you do, An?" Nathan probed as he ate. "Keep with Ju and Gui? Make sure they are alright?"

An nodded vigorously. Nathan was busy eating, but An then stared at the head of hair as the officer tackled his pork, realising this was an instruction, not a question after all. The price of his freedom.

"Yes, sir. And when you return next year, we can meet and I can let you know about our adventures. About how we have been getting on. And how well things have been with us."

"That's the spirit, An. Be an eternal optimist."

"And I have another reason for wishing to stay. A friend needs me here."

"Ah!" Nathan nodded.

An was about to give details when Gui and Ju came out. They greeted each other and sat with An and Ning. An told Ju his news excitedly.

After a moment, Ju said to Gui, "Will you play solo tonight, dear? They sail tomorrow. I wish to speak with Ning."

Gui nodded without emotion. An bade his friend Ju farewell for now. "I can see you again soon!" he told her.

"And I can tell you my other news!" So they parted with his mystery intact.

Ju and Ning held hands, laughed and chatted as they walked. When they got to the lodgings, first they stood facing one another, held each other.

Staring up into Nathan's eyes, Ju told him, "Sometimes, I want you romantically, like now. Other times, with such wild passion."

"I've noticed! And me you."

They made love.

Lying in each other's arms, Ning told her, "I could stay, like An. I could tell my father we need a local representative here permanently."

"He needs you to help get the cargoes home."

"He's not needed me for that before."

"You have to return home."

"Do I?"

"Of course."

"Well, one last time, maybe. Sort out things before coming back here. I will come back as soon as I can. Not in a year, in a few months. Winds permitting."

"Really?!" Ju brightened, the subdued mood that had been cast over the evening lifted for the first time in her lilting voice.

Neither of them mentioned being apart more. Neither of them addressed the issue of their relationship, or Ning's departure, or the achingly unknown and unknowable future.

Chapter 13

Canton, Winter 1776

Tengfei was slouching at the bar in the tavern, eyeing the dancers huddled together at a table, chopsticks poised between slender fingers, a hubbub of chatter and laughter around them. He slurped at his beer greedily. Ai was, as ever, loitering nearby. Ju appeared from the back room where the artistes prepared and joined him.

"Where's Gui?"

"Ill."

"Again?"

"Resentful."

"That suddenly Peng pays more attention to you?"

"We've known each other for a while. Why should he suddenly bother so much with me now?"

"Ai says you had a near miss."

"A very late- yes - a heavy bleed, yes - scary."

Ju glared at Ai, as if to chastise her for telling the men. But also she was furious with An, for he was the only one she had told.

"It was like a knife in his heart. That there might have been … something. His. That you were - vulnerable. Connected, too."

"Peng has a heart after all, then?"

Tengfei chuckled. "He's just a man, like any other. Like any other, we all put on a front, bravado. Beneath the mask, we're all little boys. Needing a woman's approval. Even one like Ai, maybe?"

The girl shifted uncomfortably. Her long hair hung across one side of her face. Ju wondered if it was hiding another bruised eye, though she could not quite tell.

Peng came in. It was raining outside, he shook his cape. Tengfei vanished. Ai toddled after him dutifully. Ju found herself alone with Peng.

"Want a drink?" she asked.

He nodded. She poured him a beer as the barman was out the back. The dancers had finished their meal, were sitting chatting among themselves.

"Any new songs, Ju?"

"For you to sing in Xi'an?"

"I won't sing any more of your songs, Ju, you know that. Besides, I said I'd make it up to you and I have."

"How?"

By fixing you up with gigs in Peking, Jilin City and Dandong, and a few other towns on the way back here."

"A tour? Who with?"

"Not me! Well, I will be in different venues of towns on some of the dates, so, yes, a tour all of your own."

"How!" she gasped.

"I have contacts."

"Why?"

"You are in demand, my girl. People have heard about you. People want to hear you. And your new songs."

"Really? Really?!"

"Not hard to understand why. You are … captivating."

Ju tsked. Peng reached out and fondled her breast. She shivered in unexpected anticipation, but also in reluctance.

Tengfei was on the stage, showing off to the dancers, striking up one of Peng's raunchy songs. Peng pounced over beside him, began to sing and gyrate.

Ju sipped her beer as Peng performed. Her mind wandered to home, how that warm afternoon when she was eleven and she had wandered from helping her mother and sister Mei to see if Guan-yin and Gui were able to play. She had strayed from the path to their house towards the plantation by a stream that cascaded down from one of the surrounding undulations. She heard voices near the stream, hid behind bushes, crept near.

It was Madame Lihwa's latest servant girl, fresh from Jilin. A basket on the ground beside her. Ju's father, Jia, was on the ground with her. She was feigning resistance as he groped her breasts and between her legs. But, though she turned her face from his rough mouth, she was not struggling particularly much. So Ju watched in silence and curiosity as he mounted the girl. She lay passively, panted and grunted after a time, as he did. She had seen dogs and horses do this, of course. She had overheard older village girls at the drum tower giggling about fellows, or sucking in breath at tales of errant husbands, telling who had disappointed or pleased his wife by taking a concubine. Ju left a pang of shame that her father was deceiving her mother. At the same time, she had heard the young women commenting how some married women give up on love, turn a blind eye when their men, who are more in need of *cuddling*, sought solace elsewhere. It was how folk were.

Now, Ju realised why she admired Peng so much. Truthfully, his fame and success appealed most. She knew he was a womaniser. But so were many men, they settled down. If she was with him on his travels, that would be enough for him. Her father had strayed, she knew, yet he remained loyal to her mother and she saw how Jia would always glance at his wife, Heng, with undiluted respect and devotion. It seemed to Ju that that must be the way it is between men and women. The poor men, like her father, did not have concubines because they could not afford them. Peng was no mere tea farmer, he was a famous singer, she was lucky to have his attention. Now, he was beginning to show more interest in her than ever. When he threw her a look now and again, she would smile, clap, something inside glowed.

When Peng's song had finished, Tengfei launched into another piece. But Ju winked at Peng, so that he followed her out back, to the changing room. They kissed passionately. They fucked hard.

Afterwards, Peng asked, "So, we're an item now?"

"Huh. Are we? How would I know with you?"

"I want loyalty between us. I want that. With you. To become *jiaren*. A family."

"*Jiaren*? Like Tengfei and Ai?!"

He shook his head. "Tengfei's a drunken fool. Too lazy to take a wife, running around with a slave girl to save him the bother of trying to win someone's heart. I doubt if he has a heart himself. The only things he loves are himself and the bottle. I respect you, Ju. You've always been on my mind."

"Really? Not my songs?"

"Your songs are better as yours. Unless they would suit a different voice, like the one you gave me last week."

"True."

"Besides, you're the one who's hard to pin down."

"You're doing alright now," she joked saucily, eyeing his grip on her forearms as he moved on her once more.

106

"You are the one who is enigmatic about who she prefers. Gui? That Boston man? Gang, maybe? Who else?"

Ju laughed. "You exaggerate my scope of interest. Gang?! He's old. Gui? We're friends. Ning? Didn't he sail off back to Boston, when will I ever see him again? You share my passion."

Their eyes burned into each other's like forge-reddened steel.

Chapter 14

Boston, Spring 1777

Nathan was dressed in best Sunday linen, fine gold brocade waistcoat, black shoes and white stockings, maroon breeches and matching jacket and sporting a fashionable dark, squat tricorn hat upon his neat white wig. He was walking back from church that sunny lunchtime with Miss Martha Alexander. Her pastel shoes had mid-heels and were decorated with exquisite floral designs. She had sprigs of green flowers printed on her cream dress, with orange and yellow heads. From the waist the dress billowed out stylishly, while the firm bodice slotted over bosom and waist trimly. Pale arms showed beneath frilled lace cuffs; a trim of lace covered her alabaster shoulders and chest. Martha's blonde hair was coiffured proud upon her tiny head, with a bright red bow tied snugly at the back of it.

Martha was an excellent conversationalist for someone of seventeen. She was as giggly and bubbly as her peers in society, but a little more serious and mature. They were walking to dine at her father's house, where the Grays had been invited. Their elders were walking as a group some yards ahead, chatting as they went the familiar route from the semi-rural parish church to the gates of Mr Alexander's domain.

"Lizzie and I went for a delightful picnic the other day. Tuesday, when the sun was blazing!"

"You have a mark of red beneath your eye."

"Oh! Burnt?"

"Hardly noticeable. Besides, it's natural. All the girls have caught the sun this week."

"The common girls. Do you prefer a rough sort to young ladies, Nathaniel?" Martha teased.

"I didn't mean that!" he laughed, realising they were following a side path. The laneway that led to the fruit grove. "Was it an enjoyable picnic?" he asked, thinking back to China's red-blooming bushes, the common girls there who were so natural in their friendship, compared to the stuffiness of most young ladies here or the rough sort that Martha mentioned, who were almost animalistic in their self-presentation.

"Look, the apple blossom is delightful!" Martha pointed at the trees not far ahead, with their heads of green and white. One row of pink blossom stood out.

"And the cherries are marvellous."

They paused, their shoes scrunching on the gravel path. Nathan leant forward and kissed Martha on the mouth. He tasted the dryness and greasiness of powder and rouge. He felt her hand on the back of his neck, her body press into his.

It was not the first time they had been intimate. There was an unspoken understanding between them. Which, he sensed, was about to become formalised after lunch with their families, likely with a toast from each father, a commercial union sealed as well as a romantic one.

With his eyes closed, aware of her warm hand on his skin, her mouth moving against his eagerly, her form snuggling into his, Nathan thought of how it had been while he was away. He should appreciate Martha's agreeableness, and her ardour. Yet he could not help but recall his times with Ju. This kiss was not quite like that specific way Ju's tongue would dart occasionally, pleasing him: his mouth, his tongue, his teeth, or neck, chest, nipple, stomach, manhood. Before now, in a copse like this or also here, at the fruit grove, he had canoodled with Martha. Without speaking of what they were doing, their petting had extended to his touching her, her touching him. From his experiences in China, he knew he had helped Martha achieve satisfaction, which was a rarity for girls of her background, since the fellows only cared about their own pleasure and the females were often less knowledgeable of how things could be. She had not flinched when he had placed her hand beneath his on his straining penis. She had asked, "Is this what all fellows do?" and he had nodded, so it was repeated, though he was unsure whether she was feigning coyness to avoid seeming brazen or if it was the genuine revelation he believed it to be.

Yet Nathan kept envisioning Ju: her tanned form, the tight globes of her bottom, firm curve of breast, how she would double-gasp when he licked her firm, extended nipples, how she would moan positively when he caressed her intimately. That cheeky smile she had when they were enjoying one another.

This was a brief romantic moment. They did not want to be too long reaching the house, after their families. When they got to the road, Martha's sister and brother George were passing, joined them for the rest of the short walk to the house. Lizzie giggled and Nathan and Martha knew it was because she had found them returning from a tryst.

"I was showing Nathan the gorgeous apple blossom, Lizzie. And you should see the cherry blossom now, it is out in full bloom, compared to only Tuesday."

"We can walk round later," Lizzie said with a straight face, "unless you would rather go yourselves."

"I have to go to the wharf, check on the *Firestorm*."

"On a Sunday evening?"

"There is so much to inspect, so little time to ensure all is shipshape, and the tide is at five-thirty."

"How will you cope, being away from each other for so long?"

Nathan sighed. "It will be difficult. But, at sea there is so much work to be done, just to keep afloat and heading in the right direction. Time passes quickly. Perhaps things may be different for Martha."

"I have my mare, my bridge, my viola lessons, assisting Mama running the house."

"And walking. Exploring the trails way out as far as the creeks," Nathan added.

"That far?" George was worried.

"I like the peace of the open country. The exercise."

"But the Indians ..." Lizzie objected.

"Never seen any."

"But they will have been watching you, unseen," Nathan reminded her.

"They're alright around here."

"They can't be trusted anywhere," her brother snorted.

They had reached the house. They all joined their parents and families in the dining room. Everyone was just taking their places.

Nathan heard the older ladies whispering about a scandal. One of the local mill owner's girls, Sally Hyde, had suddenly collapsed, been delivered of a child.

Esmerelda Gray told Charlotte Alexander, "These silly damsels! Well, I am proud to say I was a virgin on my wedding night and I was thirty."

James Otis was leaning across Nathan to reach the salt cellar. He butted in, "Really, Esmerelda? Unlike your sister Maria, who married that lanky pig farmer McCooke. Had a youngster three months later. Must've got himself a sow in a poke!"

Nathan's mother stared in horror at Otis's indiscretion. The other ladies' mouths opened in shock at his effrontery to insult the lady of the house.

Esmerelda stuttered, "They were very much in love."

"So your father persuaded Andy McCooke, at the point of a musket, I recall."

The ladies held back smirks, as Charlotte kindly changed the subject, and they all ignored the crudity. Nathan's eyes burned at him. Otis pulled a face, to signal back that he did not give a damn.

When the meal was over, Adam Gray walked with Nathan towards the drawing room. "Have you any announcements to make?"

Nathan nodded. Adam grinned. He spoke to Timothy Alexander for a moment, who turned and boomed, "Before the ladies withdraw to the morning room, perhaps we could all convene in the drawing room a moment." He spoke to the servants, who quickly brought flutes of white wine.

Timothy took his daughter's hand and led her to his side before the fireplace. "Friends one and all, I believe it is no secret that these two young people," he gestured for Nathan to come forward, "are fond of one another. And young Nathaniel here had come to me this weekend and declared his intentions. So, I am pleased to find such an agreeable young man engaged to be married to my darling daughter Martha. Let us toast them, Martha and Nathaniel."

They all echoed the names and drank the toast. Lizzie cheered and laughed with her sister. Nathan produced a ring and placed it on Martha's finger. They embraced and kissed, so that their mothers cooed with pride.

Timothy continued, "We all know that Nathan and his father must sail tomorrow morning on the dawn tide, to the other side of the world. What a way to begin a betrothal! But such is the nature of their trade, whereas all I have to do is take a brisk walk into town and find my desk at the bank waiting. But Nathan assures me that as soon as they return from their latest trade voyage, he will be here for a longer spell in the autumn, during which time nuptials can be celebrated."

Martha was clearly surprised by that announcement, but pleasantly so. She turned and placed her slender arms round his neck, hugged Nathan freely. The gathering broke into excited chatter as several conversations about the affair commenced.

Nathan said to his father, "I thought you weren't going to come on this trip."

It was Esmerelda who responded first. "He just had to make one last voyage. But this is definitely his last!"

"But you and Josias will still be commanding the ships, I will be aboard merely as a passenger this time."

Nathan nodded. "Perhaps on the way back I will do the same, let Richard exercise a command. After all, I may not be on all future voyages."

Adam said to Timothy and Martha, "My son is an able commander and trader. We old fellows, Timothy, need to have faith in the young and let them take responsibility. I know it's hard to relinquish the reins, but ..."

Timothy nodded.

Martha and Nathan had made their way to the French windows as the ladies began drifting out to the morning room. The sunshine was streaking bright across the grass, between the shadows of evergreens.

"We'll be alright, won't we?"

"Oh yes. Perfectly!" he assured Martha, taking her pure white hand in his, holding it reverently a moment, before raising it to his lips and pressing it there as if her skin were as delicate and adorable as a new-born baby's.

Chapter 15

Pacific Ocean, Spring 1777

Nathan reached the wheel, swaying with the ship on the rising swell, spray wetting his face, stinging his eyes. Josias was there with the lad Dando. The captain was cursing away under his breath.

"What have you done to upraise Captain Foster, Dando?" Nathan asked.

"The weather's going to slow us down. Astor's vessel's got ahead of us, they'll get out from Vancouver, beat the squall, sir."

Nathan nodded. "Blast it!" he agreed, over the growl of the gale.

"I don't like the look of this one, at all," Josias said to him. "I'm thinking of putting in at the nearest landfall."

"Aye, aye, sir, better late than never. Where is next?"

Dando was enthusiastic. "Nootka Sound, sir! The lads say it's a good run ashore!"

Nathan gave Josias a suspicious side-glance. "Uh-huh."

Josias reminded Nathan, "There's furs there. We've a lot of ginseng the natives will barter for. A fellow told me

Astor's holds are full of ginseng and beaver pelts from Missouri. We might get something better, here."

By the time they put in, the waves had eased enough so that the natives could escort them in with a flotilla of canoes. The officers and some men went with the local men to the inlet where seals were basking as a new sun rose as the winds died down. They could just walk among the creatures lazing on the rocks, clubs in hand, thumping them until their skulls cracked and blood seeped.

Two huge males stood high on their front flippers, grunting at each other, clashing heads against necks, long teeth gnashing. Two men from the *Firestorm* judged their moment to reach forward and swing at their heads, so that the sparring alpha males both collapsed in unison onto hard, cold rock. There were other species too, especially the sea otters, whose pelts were prized.

Nathan stood in awe on a high jut of rock, watching as the natives and his own men wrenched tusks from walrus heads, slit seals' bellies, sliced and hacked, stretched the skins on rough bamboo poles they had stowed below, to let them dry in the breeze and sunlight.

He did not say anything, even when Dando came over and commented, "Just think, we'll make a killing on these walrus tusks as powder for aphrodisiacs, and on these seal skins, the Chinese love 'em!"

Old Simeon was with them. He was collecting the dry furs to store in the hold and agreed, "Aye, lad, feel that – isn't it lovely? Isn't that just the most beautiful natural thing in the world, apart from a beautiful woman's skin or a chuckling infant's cheek?!"

Nathan nodded, but he was also struck silent in bemused astonishment to see the dozens of carcasses on the beach and rocks, which not long before had been an entire colony of majestic creatures, now strewn, dismembered, and bloody.

No one heard him when he vowed to the setting sun in the bright, crimson sky, "This can't be right. We will make a fortune from this. There must be another way. I can't go on like this, can I?"

As the pelts reached the ship, the native men collected their payment: knives, wood chisels, struts of iron, and sheets of tin, nails, looking-glasses and shiny buttons.

When they had gone and the *Firestorm* was nosing across the Pacific again, Nathan asked Josias, "Just how much are those pelts worth?"

"How much did we give the natives? Maybe a couple hundred dollars' worth of stuff? Astor's beaver pelts aren't worth as much as what we have. Fifteen hundred sea otter alone, at one hundred and twenty dollars a pelt. There's the seal, the rest, not to mention the tusks." Josias grinned as he raised his eyeglass and peered out at the horizon. "The wind's taking us to Fiji."

When they reached the lush, forested island of Fiji, they were greeted with the natives madly waving Union Jacks. They respectfully waved back with Stars and Stripes. The men melted away to gather round bonfires on the beach that sultry evening, hosted by the local people. The officers were invited to the enclosure before the chief's hut, for a formal dinner.

Bare-breasted women danced frantically to a pounding beat of drums as boar on spits were carved, roasted yam, glorious shapes and sizes and tastes of fruits and delicacies were brought. A missionary who had stayed there for two years and had learnt the language, Dr Gunter Neumann, translated for them.

"The chief wishes to know what goods you have to offer him."

"Please tell the chief we are honoured to be guests here, Dr Neumann. In gratitude to him," Josias said, "we bring casks of brandy, rum …"

The Chief was animated. Dr Neumann asked, "Any Chinese *sham shoo*?"

Josias and Nathan swopped incredulous stares. Nathan laughed. "We are going to China, not coming from it. But in our hold we do have a few bottles of that very good Chinese wine. He will have all that we have." Josias whispered to Dr Neumann, "Between you and me, it's cheap moonshine, but if it is to his taste, he can have it! Also," he continued, "we bring ginseng."

The Chief reacted happily when told this news. Dr Neumann told them, "The Chief is very pleased. He says his people will help you harvest sandalwood, also birds' nests …"

"Birds' nests?" Nathan asked Josias.

"The Chinese make soup with them, remember."

As Nathan was taking this in, the Chief spoke rapidly to Dr Neumann. Around them, the drum beat increased in tempo even more, the women swirled more and more, like dervishes. Neumann told him, "And the chief says he is so very pleased with what you have brought to trade, you, sir, must lie with his daughter."

The Chief had an arm outstretched to a young woman, who was taking a break from her dancing.

Nathan smiled and said to Neumann, "Thank the Chief for his kindness, but there's no need for that …"

Neumann's eyes rolled. "Mr Gray, you *must* lie with his daughter. Otherwise, it will be considered a great insult. They will wonder, is she not pretty enough, et cetera. Believe me, I have been here two years. I have seen men boiled alive for less."

Nathan smiled at the Chief and, raising his drink, replied, "I understand completely, Dr Neumann. And of course, it will be my great honour and pleasure to … fulfil the chief's wishes."

A short time later, the woman took Nathan by the hand, led him to a hut. Other serving women swished around him, removed his clothes, and even prepared him for the business at hand, all chatter and happy gestures. The island princess seized him, kissed him, and caressed him on the comfortable mats in the hut as a burning fire flickered. Nathan did his duty, took his time in ensuring she was satisfied by his attention.

But once again, as he lay beside the snoring beauty whom he knew he should feel so privileged to be with, within his heart Nathan was wondering was this a price worth paying for making a fortune?

Chapter 16

Dandong, Spring 1777

Ju was among the crowd with a couple of her friends from the troupe of dancers, clapping and singing along to Peng's songs, when Madame Fen entered the House of Raptures. She sought out Ju, went to her. Ju invited her to sit with her. Wine was brought for them. The dancers went to prepare for their performance. Fen barely sipped the wine. She had become heavier around the jowls and midriff, Ju noticed.

"Back in Dandong. Gang told me you were coming to town. How has the touring been going?"

"Brilliant! Great fun!"

"And a great success, I hear."

Ju nodded. "I can't believe it. Top billing in many places. Or second only to the likes of Peng."

"You have struck out alone. Well, without Gui, I mean."

"He had teamed up with a few others. A different type of music. We often play in the same venues, on the same nights. We all travel together at times."

"But you are in Peng's company, now."

Ju glanced from the stage and Peng's intense rendition of a love ballad to the madame. "You disapprove?"

"My dear, it is not my place to disapprove of anyone. The things others disapprove of, I profit from. I understand people's - need of various - distractions. It's just - I had hoped Ning would have been more in your thoughts."

"He went to Boston."

"He said he would be back."

Ju shrugged her shoulders.

"Ah! You young people! So impatient. A few months seems like an eternity to you, you cannot wait. Cannot commit."

Ju turned on Fen. "Commit? Me, to him? He left me. Am I to believe the word of a European? A foreign adventurer? Did he take me with him? No? Too ashamed to have a coolie wife back in Boston? Is that why his father abandoned you? The child was white enough to pass back there, but not its mother, so you were left behind?"

Fen slapped her cheek with her fan. She regretted it immediately. "Sorry, my dear!"

"It didn't hurt!"

"What you said did. Because it is true." Fen sighed. "However, I thought you cared about him. Despite his white arrogance."

"What is love, Madame Fen? For a man, I mean? You have seen enough of men to know what they want – not a woman, a particular woman, but a willing woman. Any*body* will do. So long as she is available exclusively to him, when he wishes it. That is what I have seen of men. This man, Peng, he serves me while he chooses to, it pleases him that I please him. What happens when I am tired of pleasing him? Will he seek his pleasure anyway, as so many men do, in another house, your house? How can I be sure I am loved when I am - only conditionally needed?

Why should I expect a man to be true to me, when I am not sure I can fulfil all his needs, all the time?"

"This Peng is more suitable?" Madame Fen spat.

"Is any man more suitable than another?"

"One thing I have seen from my dealings with men and women, dear Ju, is that often it is the woman's expectations that ruin the relationship. She expects perfection, yet is unable to reciprocate."

"You think your bastard son is more perfect than other men? Yet you have only met him once or twice. Where has he been for you? Where has his father been for you? What kind of a life have you had, thanks to them? Have they tried to help you any?"

"I don't need help!"

"Just as well. We may never see those Boston men again."

"You may see them sooner than you think, girl. The *Firestorm* was in Canton a fortnight ago, she docked in Dandong this afternoon."

"Well, then, they have come for the first season of tea, I would say. Rather than you or me."

"You little bitch! You won't sing in this town again!" Madame Fen leapt to her feet.

"I will tonight. I'm on now!"

Ju ran to the stage and joined Peng in a duet. Madame Fen stormed from the tavern. As she left, she stared back with angry eyes, but they were also eyes that were smarting with tears.

Gang was there, saw her in distress. He took her arm to help her out. "What's wrong, Madame, are you in pain again?"

"Oh, Gang," she shook her head. "My life has been full of so much pity and so many regrets. Once again, I see error. I despair at failure."

Had Madame Fen been a little slower in departing, she might have met the group of officers from the *Firestorm* arriving in rickshaws just along the street. Had they been a little sooner, they might have entered in time to see Peng and Ju performing their duet.

After it, the couple left the stage and went towards the bar. Peng was met by Tai, an impresario and agent from Peking. He and Peng launched into an animated discussion of a six night trip there. From their conversation, Ju picked up that the first show would be in less than a fortnight's time.

"Do we leave soon?" Ju asked Peng excitedly as Tai headed out to relieve himself, knowing the journey would take at least ten or eleven days.

He laughed. "It's only me they want. You may be a big fish in a small pond, but I'm a big fish in the biggest pond!"

Ju's jaw tightened. She stormed out to the artiste's room and slammed the door behind herself. Tai was returning to drink with Peng, so he let her go.

"What's up with the girl?"

Tengfei was joining them, carrying beers. "She wants to be the brightest star."

"Don't they all," Tai muttered. "She's good. But nothing special."

Peng responded, "She may be rough around the edges, but with a little training she will be great."

Tengfei snorted. "You'll never train that one!"

"Can any of them be trained?!" Tai agreed.

Peng scowled. "I can train them alright." He sank his beer.

"Keep a slave girl, like I do, it's the only way to ensure they obey you," Tengfei muttered into his beer. At this comment, Ai remained unemotional at his side.

"I'd like to hear the talent in the place round the corner. I hear the lads that play there are handy." Tai said.

"Gui and his mates?" Tengfei scoffed. "Alright. Nothing special."

Peng and Tengfei went out through the back with Tai, as it was a short cut to the street they were heading for.

They passed An. He was working there now, as a stage hand and general gofer. Ai slowed, parted from Tengfei and his companions, stayed to talk with An. They were passing the changing room and heard sobbing. An sensed it was Ju. He knocked gingerly on the door and he and Ai entered. Ju was sitting on a chaise longue with her face in her hands. She looked exhausted and glum.

"Hi, Ju! How are things?"

She shrugged her shoulders. "Fine, I guess. Maybe I expect too much and so am disappointed."

"That is what the Buddha says, is it not? We are slaves to our desires. When we do not get what we crave, we ache, cry. But if we strive to achieve in this material plane of existence without being too attached to the outcome, or the possessions of this world, we retain spiritual harmony. And purity."

Ju smiled sadly. "I know the theory, it is difficult to live it."

An nodded.

"I have more success than others, yet I am disappointed when I do not get more."

"It's only natural to want more." An nodded, and gently patted her arm. "Has Peng abandoned you?"

"Oh, he's off drinking with a contact in the business." She yawned.

"Yes," Ai confirmed, "they are all away to get drunk and listen to music. We can have some peace for a while."

"Go home, if you are tired," An told Ju.

"I'll wait for him. They will come back here. Peng had one last set at the end of the night."

"Rest yourself! I'm off to do so," Ai told her. "You know, you know Tengfei is not always kind." She bared her back, showed the bruises, also the backs of her thighs, several places on her body.

"The brute!" An exploded. "I'll kill him!"

Ai put a hand on his chest. "Don't get yourself in trouble!"

Ju was nodding and lay down on the chaise longue with her head on a pillow. An lifted a piece of cloth and draped it over her before he left. "Poor Ai. He must be stopped."

"He will be," An vowed.

"I thought I saw Ning in the crowd?"

"No," An told her what he knew. "They're not here yet. Another couple of days, I heard. Maybe you are dreaming of him? Want to see him?"

"Why should I? Does he think of me?" Ju's eyes closed, her head soon swirled into sleep.

An beckoned Ai from the dressing room.

In the House of Raptures, the *Firestorm*'s officers had a quick meal and some drinks. Nathan glanced around occasionally, to see if Ju might be there. He recognised Gang, standing drinking with someone, but none of the singers were familiar to him. It did not surprise him that she was not there, he did not hold out much hope that she would still be around. Or interested in him. He convinced himself that Martha was a suitable match. She seemed a compatible mate and it was only sensible that he should return home and marry respectably. If his father had engaged in a slight aberration in his youth, he had at least rectified the situation by marrying into a good connection later. Nathan's birth mother was dead or lost, had been the story. After seven years, it was only natural Adam had remarried. Nathan had six sisters, though three had died in infancy and poor Elizabeth, in her teens, was sickly. Why should he not return home and rule the family trade empire from there, as a proper American gentleman? He was growing tired of adventures and the troubling things he was seeing out in the rough world. Perhaps he wanted to retire to run the business at home, let his brothers do the voyaging in future.

"Here's Astor!" Richard hissed.

A large group of very drunk and noisy Boston men had arrived, bedraggled from the shower that had just begun. They were buying more drink and more food. John Astor was an amiable fellow and he had a reputation among the traders at Whampoa Island and further beyond for being sharp.

"He's got wind of our success last year and here he is, trying to cut in on the action."

"Which he will," Nathan replied to Josias. "He has the capacity, the capital and the guile. He'll undercut us. But he will be dead drunk tomorrow morning. We must strike immediately. Go then, get the deal done before he reaches the plantations."

His colleagues nodded determinedly.

J J Astor paused to shake hands with them all. "How's things going, Nathan?" he asked.

"Fine. We picked up some pelts and sandalwood on the way. They've sold well."

"Pelts? Our beaver fetched twenty-five dollars apiece. But we lost out on the ginseng we brought, because the Dutch beat us here and flooded the market."

Nathan nodded. "It's never easy. Always a risk."

When Astor had moved on to dine with his men, Josias and Richard stared wide-eyed at Nathan. "Only twenty-five apiece?"

Nathan assured them, "He got at least fifty-five."

"Still not as good as - what we got for the sea otter and seal."

The Gray crew toasted their success.

Peng, Tengfei and Tai had returned to watch the last act before the former two took to the stage again. Having urged Ai to go home to rest and assured her he would not do anything rash to Tengfei, An appeared from the back and went over to say hello to his former officers.

The tavern was crowded and some of the drinkers were jostling. A table with an opium pipe on it was tipped over. The flame caught spillage from a particularly volatile alcoholic beverage and some curtains near the passageway to the back and at the edge of the stage went up with a whoosh. One man's clothes caught alight. Men tried to douse him as he screamed in terror. Within a few minutes, there were several seats of fire and the blazes were so intense the heat was driving people from the tavern.

As Peng and his friends moved to leave, passing where Nathan and his friends were, An grabbed at Tengfei.

"Get off me."

"Isn't Ju still in the back room?" An demanded.

Peng told him, "She'll have gone home."

"No! She was still there."

"No one can get through there," Peng retorted, gesturing at the inferno that surrounded the passageway out to the back rooms.

Peng, Tengfei and their companions coughed and staggered to the exit. An moved towards the main fire but the heat held him back. The blaze was already raging, engulfing the stage and back area of the tavern. Without thinking, Nathan snapped off his jacket, wrapped it around his head and dived into the dancing flames that blocked the corridor.

He darted so quickly, he felt nothing. Luckily, the flames were not very deep. A few leaps forward and he was moving away from the heat again. But the corridor was filled with smoke. It was a tunnel of furnace-like heat.

Nathan heard a muffled calling: "Ning! Ning!"

Inside the artiste's room, Ju had woken coughing. Half-asleep, half-dazed by the toxic fumes, she had struggled to her feet and stumbled towards the door. The soles of her feet were burning. She was not even aware that she was crying out.

As Nathan reached the dressing room door, it was flung open from within. Ju was standing there, radiant in her white gown, eyes bulging, staring at him. Sweat was running from her brow and along her arms. The gown was stuck to her perspiring body. But they only had an instant in which to look upon one another, because the opening of the door sucked a backdraught along the corridor and into the room. With a whoosh they were buffeted into the room. The blast was like a riled dragon's breath. Ju landed on her back on the chaise longue she had just risen from; Nathan was knocked skidding across the floor and headfirst beneath the chaise longue.

He gasped as he struggled up from beneath the sofa in the dressing room. It was hot and choking with fumes. Grey swirls were replaced by another explosion that rocked him off his feet as another eruption shook the building. Through the gloom that blurred his vision, Nathan spotted Ju supine on the chaise longue. Her skin was scorched red. She was unconscious, wheezing like a done cat.

Nathan picked up the young woman and carried her out through the doorway as the raging fire encroached from the corridor, leapt up the curtains, dancing on the dressing table, cracking the artiste's mirror. He staggered with Ju in his arms to the door at the far end, avoiding the tongues of flames at either side as wallpaper and wooden walls blazed. The exit door was locked. Still holding her in his arms, Nathan kicked the door hard. It bounced back towards him, striking him on the arm, nearly making him drop Ju.

The building shook and there was a deafening roar. Nathan staggered to stay on his feet and balance Ju in his arms. There were a series of whizzes, cracks and explosions. The blasts behind them were accompanied by thuds nearby on the walls and woodwork, with blazing trails.

Nathan snatched at the body in his arms like a wayward sack of vegetables, to hold on. He staggered out into the rain as An appeared behind him, having leapt through the wall of fire. His hair was alight. There was a barrel nearby, full of rainwater – Nathan made rapid sign language for An to dip his head in this, which he did. His head hissed.

There was still the occasional rocket whizzing and banging, some even coming out through the doorway, exploding in a hiss and gasp of twinkles and sparks in the downpour. The blaze was reflected and refracted in the raindrops, so that the sky seemed to be ablaze, set off in some colourful array, like New Year lights.

Ju was retching and gasping. "What's happening?" she wanted to know. "Have I set fire to the rain?" she asked in her dazed state, for all she could see was orange, green, blue and scarlet flames leaping and seemingly devouring the steaming, smoke-billowing shower that was drizzling down on all Dandong that dark, dark night.

"The new year fireworks boxes stored near the doorway went up," An gasped.

Ju did not really hear him. She was dazed. She stared through reddened eyes at Nathan, bending over her. "Ning? Am I dreaming?"

An cried, "He's here. Really. We are here, Ju. We got you out. You'll be safe now."

An and Nathan carried Ju a few streets to An's lodgings, near Ju's own. They set her on the bed.

An said to Nathan, "There's not much we can do, except make her drink water and wait. Let her body heal itself. I can make a poultice -"

"You will nurse her?"

"By day. And when I am working, my friends will stay with her."

"I would take her on the ship, but ..."

"Sailors are superstitious about women being on board. It would not be good for her. She will be safer here. I will take care of her."

Nathan drew some coins from a money bag he had in a pocket. "This should help. If she doesn't live, give her the best funeral. If she does, tell her it was nothing but that I request the opportunity to visit her when she is well. Tell her I'm sorry, but I have to beat Astor back with the fine tea. Otherwise we are ruined. So I will see her on my return. We'll send ginseng for her."

"You are going all the way to Boston?"

"No. But one of the ships might. Or, we may be able to meet a friendly ship that is on its way here and which is happy to return swiftly, without docking in China but getting a cargo from us."

"You think of everything!" An grinned, impressed with Nathan's tactics.

"Be sure to tell her," Nathan was telling An, "to get well soon!"

Nathan hesitated. He was torn between caring for the girl and knowing he needed to sail in order to ensure the company prospered. But he went, leaving it at that.

Chapter 17

Dandong, Spring 1777

Ju's raw flesh blistered, then slowly began to peel and heal. She did not dare go out for fear of being seen. To begin with, the touch of a breeze on her skin was painful.

An nursed her with such care, gently patting her skin with lukewarm water to ease it, applying his grandmother's special poultice and wrapping lengths of cotton around Ju's burnt limbs to sooth them. He sat beside her, spooning soup and fortifying herbal drinks – more of his grandmother's potions - into her to keep her strength up when she was so wiped out, had so little energy she could scarcely rise from the waist up to take anything.

Ju's spirit was also deflated. But she would be lying there listening for a time to An's warbled attempts to sing and his versions of the comedians' jokes and tales of other artistes and what they were up to. He told her how Madame Fen had let them use a couple of rooms at the front of her place as tavern rooms. Small, but enough to keep the place going until the mess was cleared, the soot and charred debris dumped, the choking stench of smoke and sulphurous cordite from the fireworks dispelled, and the refurbishment carried out.

An carried scandal about the latest love affairs among the dancers. He even betrayed a crush on one of them and reports of his faltering progress in his quest, while she was sleeping or being minded by his friends as he was working, to seduce him.

"He has a habit of limbering up, stretching his muscles, in the space beneath the staircase. No one goes to that far end of the corridor. Except me. To pass by to get crates of beer, or crates of wine, or trays of plates and cups," An confessed. "Last night, I paused to say how great the previous night's lifts had been. He chatted with me, pleased to be appreciated! He said my hair had grown back fine and the burn scars can't be seen at all, I am my old, handsome self!"

Then, the following night, An was glum, for, of all people, he had seen Gang go out there before him, he had crept out to listen and overheard the old codger chatting with him, say how firm his muscles were. He had agreed, flexed them. Old Gang had moved forward to squeeze them, next thing he had a hand on the fellow's groin, and they were getting friendly!

"Poor An!" Ju popped up onto an elbow, to reach forward and give him a consolatory hug as he bowed his head in his hand on his lap.

An suddenly grinned. "I know. He's not worth it after all. My prince is yet to come. But, honey! Look at you, all alert, Ju! You have more energy that you let on. So! Tomorrow morning after a good night's sleep and a hearty breakfast, we get you on your feet and moving, before those gorgeous legs of yours waste away."

"Oh, I can't, yet."

"The first few times will be hardest. But we need only take a few steps."

The next morning, the greatest effort was indeed to lift her to her feet off the side of the mattress and prise that deadweight, for all Ju's petiteness, vertical. She staggered across the room, was swung round by An like a doll, flopped back on the mattress ruthlessly, but squealed in delight, "I've done it!"

Exhaustion accompanied weeks of Ju's homespun physio regime at An's direction. But the more she accomplished, the more she was determined to progress. After her first short walk out in the street, down to the stalls at the end of the street, she paused and got a snack with An. Resting there on a stool they brought out for her, back against the wall, Ju revelled in the sunshine on her cheeks. "It doesn't hurt anymore!" she basked, face heavenward. The journey uphill back was such an ordeal, she lay on her mattress panting, too breathless for some time even to drink water. But she was elated and more determined than ever.

Then, An came in one evening shaking with excitement, for he had shocking news. "Ju, darling, I'm married!"

"What!" It was the first time Ju had sat up rapidly without groans and scrunched face. "To a woman?"

"To a beautiful, delightful, wonderful female, friend, woman, yes!"

Ju dragged herself from the bed to sit with him and sip tea as he told her all at an accelerated pace.

"You know her. Ju, you are my most darlingest friend in all the world and always will be. But I also have another female best friend. And she is so lovely. The way it is between her and me, it is different to the way it is for me with any other woman. In the past, I have confessed to you the swirling emotions within in me that draw me to … others." He made nodding gestures, as if trying to head a ball, to suggest what he then admitted, by mouthing, "*Men.*" He sighed long and deeply. "Why should I content myself to be boxed by others, try to conform to whatever tea chest they want to shut me in? Life is strange, Ju. Love is a strange affair. You think you know yourself. Then suddenly you get to know someone, somewhere deep within there is a click," An snapped his fingers, "a spark ignites ... oh, sorry, Ju, dear," he touched her arm, one of the faint scars left by the conflagration in which she had almost perished, "and wallop! You realise you are in thrall to someone precious. So precious your heart is wrung like a dishcloth when you are apart. Or when they suffer."

"Who is she?"

"Ai, of course."

Following the brief silent pause, Ju summoned more than enough energy to wallop An, slapping his head and shoulders, his back as he turned from her blows. "You bloody fool! An! An, how could you?"

He stared at her wide-eyed. "Are you jealous?"

Ju slapped him again. "I'm furious! You married a slave girl? You made yourself a slave? To that bastard Tengfei?"

"To save her. You know what he was doing ..."

"It's not your place to interfere, to ruin yourself to that extent, just because you feel sorry for some wee slave girl."

"Because slaves are ten a penny?"

"How could Tengfei allow it? Ah! Of course. He is a drunkard! Easily cajoled when in his cups. Pah! An! An!" She hugged him. "My bloody fool."

"It's going to be fine. We've had the confrontation already. The sober Tengfei being told – 'Don't touch her again, she's my wife!' *'That makes you my slave, too, you damn ball-less coolie.'* 'I've more balls than you, you drunken sot, and I'll prove it if you touch her again.' *'She remains my slave, I'll fuck her when I like.'* 'You'll have to fuck me first!' *'I bloody will, I'll have your arse raw, you coolie shit!'* 'I'm waiting for you to try, big man.' Ju, darling, he'd leave her bleeding every time." Tears began to drip from An's eyes.

Ju nodded, comforted him. "Well, Tengfei will soon tire of this. He will want a new slave girl. He will want shot of you both. Before he sells you two to some even rougher stranger, I think I have an idea."

"It's not just sympathy, Ju," An told her through his tears. "Ai and I, we are..."

Through her own tears, Ju hushed him, told him, "I know. I understand."

One evening, just after dark, Madame Fen came in. An clearly expected her, though it was a surprise to Ju. An brought in a chair for her and left them alone.

"My dear, I know you've been suffering for a long time. I'm sorry I haven't been before now."

"We parted on bad terms, for which I am eternally sorry."

Fen took Ju's hand. "My girl, no. I would have been here sooner, but I have been indisposed myself."

"Oh!?"

"I went to my country home to escape the hurly-burly of town. I just couldn't face it anymore. That fire was no accident. It was orchestrated by a rival businessman. He bullied his way into getting ownership of the House of Raptures. And he wanted my other establishment also. To begin with, I resisted. When I was younger, I would have seem the likes of him off. But I have been so weak, so tired. I stalled him for a while. When I got a decent offer, I sold. So! Now I can live off my meagre savings."

"You've been unwell?"

Fen was still bloated around the face, her body was stodgier than just a year or two ago. "I have had something unpleasant within. A friend, an acupuncturist, thinks it has reduced under his treatment. I certainly feel much better after their care and much rest. Being in the country has done me good. The stresses of doing business in the throng of the city," she shook her head, "grind one down."

Ju nodded. "I can understand, when feeling low, how difficult it is to - carry on. Thank you for coming to see me, Fen."

"I came to town also, because Gang, who now works for the new owner, visited and told me the Boston ships are back in Dandong tomorrow."

"Ah! You hope to, no you *will*, see Ning. Sorry, Nathan."

"I like Ning! Yes, give him a Chinese name! Damn his Yankee father!" They laughed together.

"I like him, too."

"Yet?" Fen commented.

Ju stared at the floor. "I expect An told you it was Ning who saved me from the fire? Peng was there, like everyone else, he reckoned no one could get through that inferno, to me. I was a goner. Peng came to see me the next morning, before he left for Peking. I don't remember anything about it. An said he stared, horrified. Said his goodbyes, thinking I was dying. Said I was fun.

"An said Peng had gone round the back that night, the long way. Everyone said they don't know how any of the three of us got out, let alone got out alive. Ning acted on impulse, risked his life to try to do the impossible. The impossible was possible. I was saved because, though he had not seen me for so long, he cared, instinctively, to try to save me. To try to do the impossible. Because it was me. He maybe didn't even know what he was doing, his heart drove him to do that."

There were tears on Fen's cheeks. "Oh, my dear, Ju. Miracles do happen. The miracle of love does happen. Rarely, I grant you. And I am not sure I have seen much of the miraculous in my life. Perhaps witnessed it on a rare occasion in someone else's life. I don't believe a miracle will save me. Perhaps this illness may be staved off for a little while. But my life is one of struggle to survive, folk like me are not made for miracles."

"Perhaps you can be a miracle-worker? I have some friends need help. An, has married a slave girl, to help her."

Fen stood up abruptly. Waving a hand, she dismissed it, "There's nothing can be done about things like that. It's the way of this world and interference will only cause more trouble than it's worth. Steer clear of that, girl. But for you, dear Ju, just perhaps there is room for one miracle in your life. If so, *believe*, believe in it with all your being, embrace it, and never let it go!"

Ju looked up at her. They held hands out to hold, entwined fingers briefly before Fen began moving towards the door. "You want to believe that."

"Of course I do! I gave birth to him!" she laughed away her emotion. "Now, my girl, rest. This exercise regime An has you on will soon gather apace. It will become easier and easier to do more and more. Before you know it, you won't recall how trying or tiring it was to try to touch your toes or walk the length of a mere room. You'll be running in the sunshine like a little one again."

"I want that so much, to be by Lake Songhua again, in the summertime, with the tea bushes shiny, rich and verdant, the trees swaying in the cooling breeze, the birds chirruping merrily, the forest-side deer startled as children dive and swim. You must come to Songhua!"

"A bit far just now for me to consider, Ju dear. But soon, maybe."

Fen smiled as she drifted through the door. She waved as she left. Ju smiled back and flopped back onto her pillow. An slunk in once Fen's rickshaw could be heard clattering down the street.

"Well?" Ju patted the mattress for him to sit beside her. "Fen tells me the *Firestorm* is back."

"In the morning, I heard."

"Will you go and see if he will come to me?"

"Why don't you go to him?"

"All that way, down to the wharves?"

An jingled some coins. "Madame Fen makes it possible!"

Ju shrieked and hugged her friend in delight.

"I know," he said, "she and you like him. But ..."

"But?"

"He's a Boston man. You're a coolie."

Ju nodded. "His father - But he is a different generation."

"He's English. European. Well, American, whatever they are now."

Ju sighed. "I know. But they can't all be perfect!" she joked.

"And!" An added, "He's a man."

Ju raised her eyebrows, her expression signalling agreement there.

"And you?" she whispered.

"Well. I have learnt there is more to love and life than ... passion. Ai, for her part, has had more than enough of men's passions. And I, what need have I of much of that? We walk in the park, we sing, we act plays together, we cook, we eat. In the depths of night's darkness, we cuddle, console one another. My wife, my marriage, if it is a matter of convenience, it is most convenient. For both of us."

"Is that enough, An, darling?"

"Oh, more than enough, Ju! Most definitely!"

Ju lay back on her mattress again, exhausted. With her eyes shut, she responded, "Well, in my experience, in a year's time, if you are free of Tengfei, she will become bored of you and your inabilities. Some handsome charmer will come along and seduce her away from you. Because he can; any one can. And poor An will be left with a broken heart and regrets of having sold himself into slavery and risked his all for an ungrateful slut."

"Ai's not like that!"

"That's what they all say."

An pouted for a moment, stepping by the door like a child needing permission to go do a wee. "Well, you don't have to throw yourself through every open door, Ju. Running after scum like Peng, for what? Demeaning yourself like a bitch in heat to a scoundrel like that, even after he steals your songs, for what? For the possibility of a contact in the business, a chance of a gig in some opium den in some grotty town somewhere, full of drunken scum like Tengfei, who are more interested in their beer and the whores around them than the fact that you're whoring yourself for the chance to sit there and be ignored by them? You were better off on your own in the Songhua drum tower with only Guan-yin, Gui, me, old Duyi, the dead ancestors and the west wind to hear you."

An slammed the door as he left.

Chapter 18

Dandong and South China Sea, Early Summer, 1777

While in Dandong, Nathan had gone to see Ju, the day after her spat with An. Just before his arrival, the door had creaked open and Ai had burst in like sunshine. An was behind her, sheepish as an ogre.

"What's this about you and An rowing?" Ai demanded to know. "*He said, she said*, is all I hear. If you insulted me, maybe I deserved it? Or didn't? Who knows, who cares. I know you two are too good friends to let this nonsense fester. So, kiss and make up while I make you some tea, Ju. And An will tell you about your visitor."

An slumped onto the mattress beside her gingerly, grinned, and opened his arms. They hugged. "He'll be here from the ship in an hour. So how about we tidy you up? Or are you going to fall out with me for suggesting you look like a donkey's arse first thing in the morning?"

Ju, An and Ai laughed together.

Ju was so in such better form by the time he arrived, despite some blistering still from the fire. She was cheerful, energetic. An's words from the night before had burned on her heart as she lay awake in the night. When Ning came, she was determined to appreciate him.

She was up from her mattress when he got there. They did not speak, she moved forward, embraced him, and said, "I need to get outside!"

"I'm glad to be on firm land, too!" he assured her.

They went out for a picnic, taking a basket Ju had and filling it at stalls in the street. Ning hired a rickshaw to deliver them to the public gardens, where they walked and chatted. Ju was able to stroll all the way to the beach on that warm, sunny morning. They snuggled down together on the dunes at the deserted shoreline, both fell asleep to the sound of the gulls. There was no need to say anything: they knew, shared their sensing.

That evening, they wandered back to town and dined at the best hotel. They spent that night and the next few nights at the hotel, bathed in each other's worship. Going out to browse at the stalls, visit friends, eat at a tavern or restaurant, watch a show or listen to some band.

There were times when Ning returned to the ship or the factory, also, to work. But he spent as much time as he could with her. One afternoon, his father was looking for him at the factory.

"Where's the bloody boy now? Has he got himself tied up with some damn coolie bitch?" Adam asked the comprador who managed their factory.

Nathan emerged from behind stacked tea chests. "No, father, no need to worry on that account," he said, peering at an inventory list.

The older man harrumphed and went on his way.

When the time had come for the ship to sail, Nathan had said to Ju, "I'm sorry my work takes me away. I wish we could settle down together."

"Really? Perhaps it's meant to be for now. You have to trade, I have to sing."

"Have to? You want to, you don't have to."

"You don't have to sail."

"It's not the same thing. My business …"

"My music, my art," Ju dove an arm against her breast. "It's more than mere trade: it's a vocation. Something one just *has* to do."

"I have a duty to my family business."

"I have a duty to my - inner spirit."

"Well, perhaps it won't be long until us both fulfil our duty. Then we can be together?"

"I would like that. Someday. I think." Despite her row with An, something was still holding Ju back: despite everything, her ambition still held sway over her soul and she could not deny it.

So they had parted with a half-understanding. Now, Nathan was back into the shipboard routine. It was their fourth day at sea, since leaving Dandong. The *Firestorm* was on its way to Canton, ferrying a load of various cargoes for clients. Tiredness from long hours overseeing the running of the ship was starting to build up. He felt he was working well with Josias as captain.

This evening, he was finished his watch, had gone to his cabin to get a lie down. He had just kicked off his boots and thrown his jacket and waistcoat on the other bunk when there was a rap on the frame. The new cabin boy was hovering.

He had noticed this fellow the first morning, in Li and An's wake, as the supplies were being loaded. A trader had barrels of duck on the deck. Li had slit one open and gravel had spilt onto the boards. Li had shaken the weighted bird in the man's face. He had gotten nasty. An had loomed, lifting a barrel like it was a tea caddy. Nathan went over and shouted for the hawker to be gone with his corrupt produce. The barrels had been rolled down the gangplank after him, ducks taking their last flight out onto the water, to a chorus of wolf whistles and jeers and cackles from the men and Dockers. But Nathan hadn't seen the new cabin boy around since. Not surprising, he had been so busy.

"What is it, lad? Yu, isn't it? You're the new fellow, huh?" he asked, disinterest evident in his tone.

"I was sent with your boots, sir. And to collect the other pair to clean."

He sat up, took them without giving the lad a second thought. In the dim lamplight he inspected the handiwork. "Well polished, except for the buckle. It needs a bit more shine. Take them back and finish it properly." He threw the boots on the floor at the boy's feet and lay back on his bed, with a long breath.

He did not notice Yu lift the shirt over his head, only heard him say, "Is there anything else you'd like me to polish while I'm here, sir?"

The voice was different, the tone disrespectful to his authority and he sat up to see the breeches being lowered, a hand at either thigh. There was linen bound around the chest. There was a dark patch of pubic hair at the groin, but no privates and the hips were rounded. Nathan blinked in the low light.

"Ju?!" Of course, *her* voice.

She unwound the linen, her breasts resumed their full shape. She climbed on top of him, naked now. He embraced her, glad to touch her warm flesh.

"How the hell did you get here?"

"An smuggled me on, I stowed away in the galley for a few hours to be sure, 'til we got to sea. Then I was introduced as the new cabin boy, Yu! Like my hair cut?" She patted her shorn locks.

"You were on deck when the hawker brought those dodgy ducks."

"That was me trying to sneak on board!"

"I can't believe you've got away with it pretending to be a boy for all this time!!"

"Why not? Fooled you, didn't I?! Though it's been tiresome. And hard work! And you're so bossy."

"Officers have to be strict, otherwise everything goes to pot."

"I know. It's been nice just knowing you're nearby. I never got a chance until now to slip away, to be with you."

"It's lovely to have you here. But this is madness!" he laughed.

They made love, then lay for some hours sleeping in each other's arms, falling asleep lulled by the sound of the waves just inches from them, on the other side of the wooden bulkhead.

They were woken by Nathan's cabin-mate, Richard, shuffling in. He threw himself on his bunk without looking over. Ju had snuck beneath the sheet, tucked in at Nathan's side until he was snoring. She had rebound her breasts and dressed with speed and returned to her duties, helping An in the officers' pantry.

Nathan went for a drink of tea, grinned at her as she worked away preparing breakfasts for the men coming off watch and fortifying tea for those going on watch. He could tell An knew he knew, now, for the big eunuch winked at him.

That evening, Nathan was on watch on deck, with just the wheel mate. Yu came out, carrying a cup of tea. Nathan was perturbed at first to see the straight lines of the trousers and shirt, the shaved head, boyish face. Due to her short stature, Ju did indeed pass for a youth. But through her disguise, he could detect her femininity; and that knowledge that she was close to him, thrilled him.

Nathan said to the sailor, "The new boy is still intrigued by sundowners."

The mate said, "It's always a beautiful sight to see the sun set on an open ocean, sir. The lads are missing it, tucking into scran."

"It's their rum ration they're tucking into!" Nathan joked.

Yu went for'ard, was hidden from the view of the wheel behind a huge crate of cargo tied to the deck.

"Yes," Nathan said to the sailor, "I'll stretch my legs, too."

He wandered to the rail, then forward. Over his shoulder, he saw that the sailor was not watching him. He stepped over to where Ju was. They thrust themselves together, kissed, and held on tight, breathing the warmth of life against each other's neck.

"I love you so much!" he whispered to her.

"Do you? I love being with you, I love you, too, darling."

"You're special."

"No, I'm not."

"Yes, you are!"

"You're a very interesting, special man, Ning. I am just a would-be singer."

"You are a world class singer."

"No, I'm not!"

"Well, you should be recognised as such, because you are. But, just, you are an amazing woman."

"But am I an interesting boy?"

For your sake, I hope not, now we've been at sea five days and the men will be getting restless!"

Nathan discreetly arranged for Ju to go ashore in Canton with An as soon as they reached Whampoa Island. She stood on deck with Nathan as they sailed up the Pearl River, enthralled by the busy-ness of the estuary. Trading ships from all nations were lined up, loading and unloading, or waiting for their chops to do so.

The hand who had been on watch the other night whispered to An, "Mr Gray's getting very cosy with the new cabin boy. I didn't think he was like Mr Hume."

An snapped back, "It's a paternal affection, that's all. We rescued the boy from a fate worse than death on the streets when we pressed him."

The seaman nodded, accepting the explanation. An allowed himself a private sigh of relief.

As she was about to go ashore, he sidled over to her and said, "It's been an interesting voyage. But let's not risk it again."

She nodded. "If that's a calm journey, I wouldn't like to be aboard when it's stormy. My poor stomach ..."

That first night ashore, Nathan met her at the hotel.

"Good news!" she told him, in the lobby, wearing a gorgeous green silk dress, fabulous earrings, sensual make-up and, to his surprise, hair extensions.

"The hair must have cost a fortune!"

"An has a friend who is a hairdresser, she lent these extensions to me. And there's a favour I wish to ask of you."

She told him of Ai and An's plight.

Ning told her, "Tengfei drinks in the tavern most nights. He's likely to be there now? Let's go see."

So they walked the short distance to the inn. Tengfei was indeed there, with Ai beside him on a stool. Ju hung back near the door.

Nathan put an arm around Ai, kissed her passionately on the lips. Tengfei sat bolt upright.

"Have you finished with this one, yet? I fancy her. How much? Ten dollars?"

"Ten?!" Tengfei sat back down again. "Maybe twelve. But you would have to take her troublesome husband, too."

"Husband? You let your slaves marry? How kind. But really, I only want the girl."

"They come as a lot," Tengfei slurred.

Nathan sighed. "What'll we do with the old man, honey?" he asked Ai. "I could sell him off."

She was about to object, when Tengfei shushed her harshly. He held out his hand. "What you do with them when they're yours is up to you. But they go together."

Nathan handed him twelve coins. He walked away arm in arm with Ai. Tengfei raised his beer to his lips, pocketing the money. Nathan and Ai went out with Ju.

In the street, Ai stared at Ju and Nathan in turn.

Nathan told her, "You and An are my slaves now. And now, you are both free. We're off to dinner. Enjoy your evening, Ai. And the rest of your lives."

They walked back towards the hotel, with Ai staring after them in surprise.

As they got back to the hotel, Ju said to him, "Thank you for that!"

He shrugged his shoulders. "It was the right thing to do."

"But twelve dollars!"

"It's only money. What use is it unless it does some good?"

As they entered the hotel again and took the carpeted stairs to their room, Ju said to him, "My news! Already I have found a venue who has auditioned me, this afternoon while you were unloading cargo, and I am to sing in two nights' time."

"Brilliant! I told you, Ju, you're a star. You sing so well."

"My lungs are holding up, after the fire, the black gunge seems to have cleared."

As they crossed the threshold of their room, Nathan said to Ju, "Mine, too. But, Ju, my dearest, while I want you to succeed in the theatres and taverns, I also have another proposal to make to you. Let's get married."

"Us? Now?"

"Soon. When it suits you."

Ju did not pause long. "Yes!"

"Yes? Just like that?"

Ju's laughing made Nathan laugh. They were soon embracing, falling onto the bed, making love with ineffable tenderness.

Chapter 19

Songhua, Early Summer, 1777

Ju was in the field, picking a basketful of leaves from the tea bush. Some for the house. She saw the dust of carriage wheels in the distance, shaded her eyes with a cupped hand. She did not recognise the vehicle or driver. As it approached, it slowed and she could see a European gentleman was being brought here. Ju was clambering back up onto the road from the field when the carriage drew level with her and stopped.

She was surprised when the old foreigner spoke to her in reasonably good Chinese. "Young woman, is this Songhua?"

"Yes, sir."

"Tell me, where can I find Jia's house?"

Ju started. Her arm rose automatically, she pointed towards the house not far away. "Here. But, why do you want my father?"

His head cocked. "Jia? Which daughter are you?"

"I'm Ju."

"Then it's you I have come to see."

He got out of the carriage, grunting with stiffness after so much time rocking in the tight-sprung vehicle.

"Why me? Who are you?"

As she asked, she noticed his looks and realised, just as he said it: "I'm Gray. It's my son who has lost his head over you." He looked her up and down. He sighed. "I can see why. I fell for a local girl when I was a young fool, and you're even prettier. I thought Nathaniel was wise enough not to make the same mistake."

"What may have been a mistake for you may not be a mistake for him."

"My girl, it's always a mistake. The power of what other people think is …"

"Not worth a fig!"

He laughed. "Easy said, girl. But it's a reality. I don't need told that."

"Now I understand more about why you disappointed Fen."

"F-? You've done your homework."

"She's still around."

"So I've heard. Gets around quite a bit."

"Because you abandoned her?"

"It was more complicated than that. But I don't have to explain myself to you. And I'm certainly not here to stir up the past. It is present circumstances I'm here to see you about."

"You don't want us to marry?"

"You *will not* marry my son."

"It's our decision."

Adam nodded. "I'm not one for hysterics. Decisions carry with them consequences. So, between you and me, we strike a deal, that results in a good deal for us both, and you say nothing to Nathaniel about it, he thinks you've decided it's for the best. He nurses a broken heart for a while. Goes home and marries his fiancée, Martha as he ought - Ah! From the look on your face I can tell that's a little secret he hasn't shared with you? And you thought you knew everything? A proper Boston lady, daughter of a wealthy banker. Now you're wondering, was he going to do what I did? Have a wife here, and another back in America? At least I waited the legal seven years before remarrying. From what I've seen, he's been having his cake and eating it."

Ju's face muscles all hardened. She could not prevent her eyes from watering. "I'm sure he has given up this Martha, in his heart."

Adam shook his head. "If he had, he'd have mentioned it to me, confessed it to you. The deal I'm offering, sweet pea, is, you walk away. Here," he threw a leather pouch at her feet. "Thirty dollars to help you go sing somewhere far away for a good while. Peking, maybe?"

"That's a crude insult. You come here, stand by the side of the road, and invade my home place, with these kind of threats …? Take yourself off!"

"Threats? I can do those as well. How about, you drop him, girl, or it comes out that he is not my son. He is Joseph Hearty's son."

"What? Who?"

"My first mate. The captain of my other ship, for years. He was as much in Fen's bed as I was, from what I now know."

"In later years, maybe …"

"Maybe? Nathaniel is said to be Hearty's child, not mine. He is disinherited. I have two other sons, sons of my *real* wife. Full-blood American boys. Nathaniel stays here with you, goes native. And you live happily ever after, the sweet romantic dream, picking tea leaves for the rest of your lives, like the pair of coolies you are!"

Ju was so flustered by Adam's vicious threat, she blustered, "You'd do that to your own son? You don't care what the truth is, you'd risk lying, ruin his life, disown him, just to spite me? I'm not a gold-digger, Mr Gray."

"You don't have to be, honey. You know you're different races."

"My family has the wedding arranged."

"We're going to talk with your father now. You will explain. How you have cold feet. You can't marry an American, it's not right. I came to meet him, but I understand. I see you are out expenses for the preparations, I help you out." He picked up the leather pouch and forced it into Ju's hand.

Ju found herself walking beside Mr Gray towards the house. The carriage trundled behind them, once the driver had got the horses' heads out of their nosebags. Ju was in tears when she reached the house. Heng was first to see her appear, called her father out. Jia sent Heng back inside, for he knew the Boston gentleman's presence spelt trouble.

Adam shook hands with Jia. "I am Nathaniel's father. Your daughter is upset. The reality of the marriage seems to be striking her, now." The leather pouch now passed into his hand. Jia glanced at it as they spoke.

"Such a change is daunting, for young people."

"Some more than others. Young lady, you told me you had something to tell your father?"

Ju stared at Jia through blurred eyes. "I don't know what I was thinking. How could I marry a Boston man? It's impossible!"

Jia roared. "You little bitch! This gentleman comes all the way here, from Canton, not just from Dandong, for you to reject his beloved son?! Is he not good enough for you? Who do you think you are? You wish to disgrace me, and your whole family? Make us laughing stocks in front of the whole village?"

"Don't be so hard on her, sir," Adam interceded. "It's better to realise a mistake now, than at some stage when it's too late. As you can see, I can help you out with the expenses."

Jia calmed to speak to Adam. "I thank you for your unnecessary kindness, sir. It's not a matter of expense. It's a matter of honour. The family name will be mud if there's not a wedding." Jia turned to Ju. "You have to make a choice, Ju. At least to say you preferred one man to another, one was more suitable. Like a local fellow -"

Ju looked up, horrified to realise the enormity of what her father was proposing. He wanted a name? Some village boy? She blinked at him, dumbfounded.

"That lad of Kun's you went to the city with, Gui. You've always been friends with him. You lived in the city together. He was telling me the other day, he's had his fill of traipsing round, one tavern after another, all the same, one town after another, all the same. Time to settle down. A quiet village like this is lovely compared to noisy, busy cities. He will work hard in his father's tea growing fields. We could join together, build up a fine enterprise …"

Ju choked. "Gui?" A friend, she thought. An arranged marriage. Well, most were. She could get on with him. They had shared their youthful adventure in the cities and taverns. "I still have ambitions. I enjoy singing …"

Jia waved a hand, dismissing her objections. "You can sing in the drum tower all day long. You are a woman, not a girl, Ju. If you don't have children soon, you will regret it. You will be left as an old maid, like Madame Lihwa."

Ju glared at Adam Gray. She knew she was beaten. "I suppose, if he would agree …" She hung her head.

Jia smiled. "I will speak to his father. I think there will be no objections. I know Gui always speaks of you, Ju. As a man, I see the glint in his eye when he speaks of or looks at you. He likes you. More than he knows, maybe. He looked after you in all these big cities, didn't he? Who brought you home after you were injured in that awful fire?"

Ju sighed loudly. She glared fiercely at Adam, then stomped away towards the house, to go and lie down on her bed and toss and turn on it, exhausted, ravaged by shock and confusion.

Jia stared at Adam Gray. "This is for the better. I know you will be disappointed, sir, that my daughter has let your son down. Will you let him have her apologies?"

Adam nodded. He tipped some coins into Jia's fist. Gray walked over to a tree, unbuttoned his breeches, pissed. "You have been put out by my son's … rashness. You are right, Jia, this is for the best, for all concerned." When he was finished, he stood before Jia, buttoning up. They bowed to one another. Gray strode over to the carriage, climbed up into it and was driven off, without another look or word.

Jia hurried across the village to his neighbour's house. Gui was there with his parents. Jia gave them the short version of the proposal – Ju realised her mistake, realised who she really preferred. The agreement was made by them all, without a second thought.

When Jia went back into his own house, Heng and Hua were comforting the expressionless Ju on her bed. "What has she told you?" he asked them.

"She won't tell us anything," Heng cried.

"She has changed her mind. That's all. Not the foreigner. She is to marry Kun's boy."

With that, Hua came running back, Gui was here. Heng stood up, mystified. Jia led her out. "You're still getting a wedding. She's getting a proper husband."

Heng nodded. "You're a clever man, Jia. Thank the gods this has happened!"

Jia wagged a finger for Heng and Hua to accompany him on a walk, up past the drum tower, towards the river.

At first, Gui had sat cross-legged on the mattress next to the silent, motionless Ju. When he was sure her family had gone, he said simply, "I know we did not treat each other the way … this situation calls for, when we were away from here. But I have realised my mistakes. I haven't met any girl as sensible as you. I do care about you, Ju. We know each other. It can work. I know," he tried to explain, "I didn't see you when you were ill, after the fire. I thought I had a chance of a gig in Peking. We went all the way there, spent so much, for a few songs in a fourth rate dive."

"I know. It was worth a try, Gui."

Her hand sought his. Ju held Gui's hand for a long time. A finger tapped the back of his hand, comfortingly. Gui was close, his thigh against hers. She felt his trousers stirring. She placed her hand there.

"You're excited."

"See: I *do* care. But will you?"

Ju patted his lump playfully. "Don't worry. I'm easily pleased. You need help, though, hm? *Husband*?"

She took out his stiff penis, worked him to the point of no return. She quickly edged her nankeen trousers to her ankles, spread her knees, let him enter her, lay there letting him work himself into a frenzy upon her. When he had finished and got off her, she smeared his come away with the sheet and rearranged her own clothes.

When Gui had caught his breath again, was fixing his clothes, he asked her, "Will you be alright, though? About everything?"

"I'll be alright," she said. "As Fen said, who expects miracles, anyway? Life's not like that, is it?" She bolted to her feet. "'C'mon. My sister Mei will be here soon, with her husband and the new baby. And the others will be back from their walk."

Chapter 20

Songhua, Early Summer, 1777

Adam was in the coach heading for the village of Songhua again, just a couple of days after his last trip. Nathan had disappeared overnight.

When Adam arrived, he walked from the edge of the village to the drum tower. The bells and drums were already sounding. He found the groom's party there. He had just got there when Dewei came running breathlessly to Gui's father, Kun.

"Ju's gone!"

"What? Where is she?"

"Not in her bed!"

Adam knew instantly that Nathan had something to do with it. He saw the men looking at him. He marched over to Gui's father.

"This shouldn't have happened. I'll do all I can to help."

A local woman came to them. "Are you looking for the European and the girl? I saw them ride off towards the drying barn," she pointed. "He had a horse. The girl seemed to be struggling."

A couple of men borrowed horses. One, the local constable, Zhou, and Kun went to Jia's house. As they left, Adam shouted to them, "If he gives you trouble, if you have to hurt him, then you must." He leapt into the carriage and ordered it the long way round to the wooden shed.

Nathan had been told the news about Ju's change of heart by messenger from Songhua, to keep Adam out of it. He knew something was up. He had sat restlessly for a while, until he could stick it no more, then got himself a horse from a fellow he knew and ridden northwards.

He had arrived at dawn. He tied the horse at the stream at the back of Jia's tea fields. He had simply crept into the house and peered into the bedrooms. The parents were sleeping in the first one. He moved on and found Ju. He seized her with a hand over her mouth and twisted an arm behind her back. He frogmarched her out, all the way to the stream, before letting her go.

Before releasing her, he said, "I'm sorry if I'm hurting you. Don't make a sound, just tell me what's going on."

Ju stepped back, stooped, rubbing her arm. "I can't marry you. You know why."

"Why!?"

"It doesn't make sense."

"That's not it."

"Yes it is."

An old woman was coming along the road, over the crest of the nearby hill. Nathan lifted the petite Ju, set her on the horse, leapt on behind her.

"Don't do this, Ning!"

"Sssh!"

She struggled as he reined the horse and spurred it on apace past the local woman, who would later bear witness to the wedding guests.

It was only a short distance until the barn appeared, which he had noticed on his way. He rode across the field, between rows of tea bushes, to the shed at the end. Ju glanced at the landscape of her homeland beyond the row of pine trees behind the barn, the hills, river to the lake, drum tower, village all radiant in the first light of morning, the houses and wisps of smoke from chimneys so diminutive upon the vast slice of earth before her as they cantered forth; and as she did so, Ju's heart ballooned with pleasure that she was with Ning and there was the possibility that they could be together forever. But even as Nathan leapt off the horse and hauled Ju from it, the other reality weighed on her soul and so she resisted his tugs. He squeezed his hands around her arms and backed her into the barn.

"The truth?"

"I am marrying Gui today."

"Gui?!"

"It is our custom, to arrange marriages that suit our families."

"*We* are supposed to be marrying today."

She shook her head. "An impossible dream." Ju tried to walk past him. He stood in her way. She stared up into his eyes through a few tears. "My mind's made up. I know what I have to do. I'm going to marry Gui."

"That's not what you *want* to do."

"I can, I know I can do so. Who does what they want to?" She tried to get by him again.

"Many people."

"In Boston? Really? Not even there, I think you'll find. If you married me, how long would it last? A couple of years? Like your father and Fen? Then you'd be sick of me and be off back to Boston, too."

His face clenched, as did a hand. "I'm not him."

"He was *right*, Ning. These things never work."

Suddenly, she leapt off the ground and thumped him in the groin with both feet. She sprang to her feet like a cat from the fall after her flying kick, while he was still rolling on the ground. His arm swung, his fingers grasped, touched the edge of her clothing but missed catching her as she darted out and vaulted onto the horse. She kicked and rode.

Nathan ran after her. Ju rode zigzag, a circuitous route, first away from home, then back round towards it. As she approached the house, she could see her young brother Dewei running off in the distance, along the road towards the village centre. Ju halted the horse outside the house. Heng and Jia came running out. Mei followed, baby in her arms.

"What did he do to you?" Heng barked.

"I'm alright. We talked, that's all. I told him this is the way it has to be. He won't bother me again. Come on, let's get ready for this wedding."

As the women went in to prepare and dress, Jia jogged after his son towards the drum tower. He only got a few yards when Kun and the other man reached him, on horses. The other man hauled Jia up and they rode off to search.

When Jia, Zhou and Kun were riding towards the barn, they encountered Nathan stumbling from the tea plantation. Adam's carriage came in a dust cloud as Zhou manacled the quarrelsome Nathan Gray, with his comrades' help.

Adam stood beside his carriage as Zhou informed Nathan he was going to be held in the cells in the village until the following morning. He would get water, food, fresh straw to lie on. Nathan stared at his father as they walked him behind a horse to the village. Adam watched him go, then instructed his driver to return to Dandong. The carriage was soon a dot of dust drifting over the horizon among the undulating land of bushes and trees.

Adam noticed a horse ride past his coach, but he did not notice its rider. With a hat pulled low over his face, the stranger rode to the village. He dismounted near the drum tower. He asked one of the local fellows was it the Boston man who was getting married. The man shook his head. He told him the story, that the girl was marrying her childhood sweetheart, a foreigner had come and tried to abduct her, had kidnapped her and tried to seduce her in a barn, but the constable had rescued her from the mad foreign devil. He asked where the stranger was now and was told he was locked in the gaol house. A finger pointed down past the most unkempt of all Songhua's streets and past the shambles.

The stranger tied his horse and sauntered to the street where the stalls ran with blood and smelt foul. When he reached the gaol house, there was no guard. Zhou had gone, with everyone else, to watch the wedding and join in the celebrations. The keys hung on a nail driven into the lintel.

The stranger strode in and peeled off his broad-brimmed hat. "Nathan?"

The figure in the dimness behind the iron bars shuffled forward. "You?!"

Nathan's surprise was so immense because the man who stood before him, white hair astray on his head, was Joseph Hearty. "Yes, I know. I'm not a ghost. I'm real. I got washed ashore at a fishing village near Jilin, Xingfu Hua-yuan. The locals nursed me for a week, till I recovered strength. A widow woman, Lei Zu. I'd a bump on my head, must've got a whack going off the ship. They found the two of us lying on a raft of driftwood. Only I survived. I couldn't remember much for a while. But I will always recall vividly my trip the Heaven, to the Land of Bliss. I swear, lad, I met my dead grandparents, they stepped forward, radiant as angels, to greet me. Saint Gabriel was with them, and Saint Christopher. And then my mother appeared," he choked back emotion. "How I wanted to stay there. But the saints told me my time on this earth was not yet at an end. People will say I'm mad, to think it was real. It doesn't take up much time in the telling, but it seemed I was there in Heaven for an eternity. And I knew, just knew, all the secrets of the ages and eternity. Ah, but how to describe it, tell it all, I just haven't the words, my lad. Next thing I knew, I was coughing up brine in a dark hut in Xingfu Hua-yuan. And the lovely Lei Zu fussing over me.

"I was loath to leave there, too. But I thought, once I got my strength back, I should try to return. They told me in Dandong the ships would be back in the spring. I didn't see the point in going all the way to Canton, waited till you came up this direction again. When I went to find the ship, they said Adam and you had come to this village, you were getting married. I wanted to be here for the big occasion, didn't expect to find all this palaver." As he spoke, Joseph unlocked the cell door and let Nathan out.

"What's the story, son?"

Nathan embraced the man, kissed him harshly on the cheek. "I was to marry a local girl. Now, they have arranged for her to marry a local fellow."

Joseph nodded. "Look, when in Rome and all that. Don't interfere any more, Nathan. These people have their own way of doing things. If the fathers have arranged a match, leave them to it."

Nathan sighed. He stretched his back, drew in a lungful of fresh air. "One last try. I will find her father, if it's not too late. See if I can talk him into changing his mind. A long shot, I know. But I just want to try it, to give me peace of mind."

Joseph nodded. "I doubt if it will do any good. But …"

They walked to the drum tower. As they did so, Zhou spotted his prisoner at large. He strode over to them.

"You should be behind bars."

"He wouldn't cause any more trouble. He's just going to apologise to her father and we're leaving."

Zhou sized up Joseph. He nodded gravely. He pointed up to the balcony around the interior of the drum tower. Jia was there, with Kun's sons, waiting for the womenfolk to arrive. Gui was with his friend and other family at the front of the main space, with the priest. Heng and Hua were there, showing off the new family member, their granddaughter and niece.

Nathan and Joseph climbed the stairs to the balcony. At the top, they passed Mei and her husband. Kun was heading downstairs now, anxious to get the ceremony over with. The drum was reverberating slowly, each thump marking the procession of the bride from her home into the village. Jia was following him.

Nathan was soon at Jia's side, at the top of the rough, wooden staircase. Jia was shocked to see the young Boston gentleman, knowing he had been locked up. Behind them, Gui's brothers were joking, shoving each other, spilling their beer as they horsed around, and squeezing past them to descend for the ceremony.

"How dare you come here!" Jia started.

"I just want to ask you once, to reconsider. Let Ju choose freely. If she chooses him, fine, I'll go. But please …"

Jia began wagging a finger under Nathan's nose. A cheer went up downstairs from Ju and her friends in the bridal party were just arriving outside, were about to enter.

164

Jia would be going down to stand with his family shortly. He was about to launch a tirade of abuse at Nathan for being there and tell him to get himself away, out the back, unseen by Ju, when he lunged forward. Nathan grabbed at him, but Jia fell against the wooden railing. He was gone. Down the stairs in an ugly tumble.

Joseph turned to see Nathan staring over the railing. Heng and Mei rushed down the stairs to him. A crowd gathered. Ju rushed in, was comforted by friends.

Nathan found himself surrounded by local men when he reached the bottom of the stairs. One growled, "I saw him push Jia!"

Zhou had him seized and returned to the cell. Joseph did not have time to raise a defence: he was ushered to his horse by angry friends of the poor man, brandishing sticks, and seen on his way from Songhua.

Joseph had been there long enough to know Jia's neck was broken. He had twitched on the ground a little while, but stilled. Heng, Mei, Ju and Hua were distraught. Dewei had raced to the gaol with a pointed stick, wanting to stab Nathan to death. He could not reach far enough through the bars, was dragged away by Zhou and his deputies.

Joseph Hearty rode to Dandong. He stabled his horse and boarded the *Firepower*. Once again, sailors crossed themselves as he appeared before them; everyone stood back in awe as he went down to Captain Gray's cabin. He told his tale of survival, then of Nathan's misfortune.

"What's to be done?" Adam demanded.

Joseph advised. "We can get the Hong merchant to find a decent lawyer. You know this country, sir, nothing moves rapidly. He could fester in a rat-hole for years."

Adam nodded. When Joseph had left him with the two empty Brandy glasses, Adam buried his face in his hands at his desk and wept.

Chapter 21

Jilin, Christmas, 1778

Nathan shared a cold, dark, dank cell with a man they told him was a local petty thief, Bao. Bao wore plain nankeen trousers and shirt, the customary queue hair crop, shaven at the forehead, long dark locks tied back in a braid. His only distinguishing feature was the white cotton cummerbund he always wore. He had not much conversation much of the time, but at least it improved Nathan's Chinese even more, having only him to talk to when he did offer conversation. After a year and a half in the gaol house in Jilin, Nathan was thin and angry.

He spent his days exercising. He was allowed to the yard for an hour a day. The others, like his cellmate, would wander about, or sit in the sun, chat, even fight. Nathan just jogged. Round and round the yard, irritating the others with the dust he kicked up when it was dry.

"Why do you run every day? You could talk to the others."

"I can talk when I'm inside. Don't we all yap from cell to cell when the guards are having their meals or their women in? I only get one hour out, so I keep myself healthy by running."

"Healthy for what?"

"For when I get out."

"Pah!" Bao scoffed. "You're on a murder charge. You are to be executed. For the first few years I was like you, too, keen to keep alive, keep up my hopes. Four years, now, and still they keep me waiting. For the end. Why bother running? Unless," he whispered, with sudden energy, "you plan to escape? Can I be in on it?"

"I don't have a plan," Nathan told him, not trusting he would not sell out to the guards. If he had a plan, which he did not. Though he was always on the look-out for ways and means, any opportunity, long- or short-term to do so. "I'm innocent," he told Bao. "Justice will prevail."

"You were found guilty in the court," Bao reminded him. "People testified you pushed that old geezer off that balcony."

"I don't know how," Nathan said, staring through the high bars at the sky beyond, "but someday the truth will be known. And I will be vindicated."

"As a corpse!" Bao sniggered. And Nathan laughed with him, only half-believing his own eternal optimism.

"Why are you here?" Nathan asked directly, for the first time.

"Thievery, didn't they tell you? What they don't want to tell you is, I should be released as a political prisoner." He patted the white cummerbund. "White Lotus Society," he whispered. "I played my part in the rebellion."

"By stealing?"

"We needed supplies. We're poor. Why are we poor? Because the elite keep the wealth of the nation to themselves."

Nathan asked, "You want to play Robin Hood, take from the rich and give to the poor?"

"When we do so, it's called theft. When it's the other way round, it's called taxation. I only took for the sake of the cause; but other comrades took for themselves. I'm the one in here; where are they? Out looking after themselves still," Bao said bitterly.

Nathan shook his head, lying back on his bunk. "We've had our fair share of colonialist massacres in Boston. A friend of ours was shot by the redcoats in one. But folk need incentive; from what I can see, free trade's the only way an economy can operate efficiently."

"There has to be some balance. There has to be some - compassion. Let everyone live comfortably. There's only so many hours in the day. The poor work as hard as, harder as, the rich. They contribute. Yet they struggle to make ends meet. I'd one drought wipe out my crops. Two of our children died in the famine that followed. The rich sat in their mansions and did nothing. Didn't even share their food. I joined the rebellion for my family's sake, for my wife and other children. And for those like us."

Nathan nodded. "It's not fair."

"We can do something about it."

"I hope so," Nathan sighed.

He was still suspicious of his cellmate, but after that, Nathan adopted the traditional queue. He asked Bao to call him Ning. Soon, the others all did so, too, even some of the guards. In his nankeen uniform, he was soon difficult to distinguish from the other coolie inmates.

One day, when the guards came to take them out, in the coldness of December, Bao was told to go out but Nathan would be kept in for the next yard session. The inmates were let out in batches, not all together. He worried for a moment, were they plotting something, like taking him out for a swift execution or delivering him into the hands of some vicious inmate who would slit his throat.

An and Li walked in to the cell. They squatted down beside Nathan, on the aged straw. "Hello, sir! Long time no see!" An slapped him on the shoulder.

"What on earth!" Nathan was so surprised to see a friendly face after so long, he wept.

Li was his usual quiet self. But he handed over from under his clothes a bottle of beer, cold slices each of chicken and ham and a large hunk of cake, all of which Nathan devoured.

"They let us come. I have a letter for you, from Madame Fen. But first, *our* news! In fact, first, how are you?"

"Fine. I keep fit. I exercise my muscles, as we do on the deck at sea. I run, not round the ship, round the yard. The Chief has some books in English an old missionary priest left in the local village. So, I have a Bible and some Shakespeare and a few other bits and pieces. The neighbours are great craic."

An laughed wildly, his big frame shaking where he was perched against the wall. "Li's ship, the *Firestorm*, is in Jilin. Captain Richard sent us to see you. Captain Joseph and Captain Adam remain in Canton with the *Firepower*. But he sends his regards."

"He wouldn't come?"

"It would break his heart to see you here, sir. And he is older, less able to stick a long journey. Captain Joseph was all eager to come, but Captain Adam forbade it. Joseph has got married."

"Married? Joseph?"

"To Lei Zu, from the fishing port he was washed ashore at, who helped save his life. Captain Adam is afire with rage that he chose to marry a coolie. And without

169

permission. Joseph said he's the captain of his ship, so he had the authority to permit himself to do so! So, he is demoted. I think he may jump ship, go to Astor's crew. But your father continues to fund the lawyer, trying appeals. They have appealed to the Emperor."

"That's bad news," Nathan replied. "Because that's the last resort. That means, once it fails, it wouldn't be long until I'm for the chop. It'll all be over by Easter."

"Don't be disheartened. The Emperor can be merciful, especially to foreigners. You're the son of a Boston trader, he will feel you have done enough time for your sins and pardon you."

"And have a whole village up in arms for justice?"

"You'll be spirited out of the country. They will think you were executed. It will all be forgotten about."

"Anyway, An, how did you team up again with this reprobate Li? Are you back at sea?"

"Oh, no, sir. I have been getting married, too. To Ai."

"And how is that going?"

"Most excellently! And we have been touring. With - with Ju. She's a big star now. She's on an extended run at the Celestial Theatre in Peking!"

"She's made the big time?!"

"Not half," Li told him. "She has a big house in Songhua, more land there, for her brother to grow tea on, property in Peking, Dandong and Jilin, and an estate out beyond Canton. Her sister and brother-in-law, Yong, runs it. And her own carriages for touring."

"Goodness!" was all Nathan could reply with. "Well," he sighed, "her association with Peng has done her good."

"Peng?" An scoffed. "He does the same venues he always did. His star has waned a bit. They aren't in the same league at all, anymore. He is still a big fish in a small pond but Ju, my mistress, is higher than he'll ever be."

"Is she happy?"

An paused, thought deeply for a moment. "She is cheerful. She works. She is alone, her life is … she is surrounded by friends, family when she can. Perhaps an occasional lover, I don't know for sure about that. But a true friend? No one gets close," he shook his head. "There is an emptiness there …"

The guard clanged open the cell door. "Time's up!"

An pulled the letter from a pocket and shoved it into Nathan's hand. As they were leaving the cell, An said to him, "Don't despair of your father. He does think and speak of you all the time. He does care, still, always. He and Mr Wu are doing all they can to help."

"I need a miracle, I think!" Nathan replied as they disappeared up the corridor towards the light at the exit.

"We're praying for you!" An shouted back. And they were gone.

Nathan was ushered out to the yard for his hour, so gripped the letter tightly while he ran. When he returned to the cell, Bao was dozing. Nathan had hidden a sliver of ham and a little piece of chicken in a crevice in the wall where he knew the ants and mice could not reach. He retrieved these and gave them to Bao. Bao stared at him with incredulity, then nibbled them slowly, to savour them for as long as possible.

Nathan sat against the wall where the narrow beam of light from the high, barred window was cast across the stone floor and took out his letter from Fen. As he read, he could picture her at her desk in her back office at the brothel, though he knew, as An had told him before the end of the trial eighteen months ago, that she had sold up her business and was now retired to a small house on the outskirts of Dandong.

"My dear son Nathaniel – Ning, as I like to call you. I hope saying that does not make you sorrowful, as I know Ju called you that. But she and I shared a friendship, despite its ups and downs at first. And I like that pet name she has for you.

"I cannot give you much news of her. The fellow An came to me to say he was going to see you, so I asked him to bring this letter, perhaps he will have more news of Ju than I do. All I know is, she is in Peking mostly nowadays, has become a celebrated singer in the capital.

"I do not believe you deliberately killed her father. We did argue about that, she and I. Even if it was an accident, she is resentful, which is only natural and to be expected. I am sorry it did not work out between you. She is such a lovely girl. I am surprised at myself for writing this, for at first I doubted her, and your attraction to her. Now, as death approaches and ushers with it a greater spiritual insight, I sense there was a more cosmic connection between you than perhaps you even realise yourselves. Though others may flit in and out of your lives, I suspect, though your relationship with one another may be stormy at times, it will endure all hardships, any misunderstandings and disagreements, any separations however long, for you are so close to each other's hearts. You are both good, realistic people. Though others may seem to be important, caring, or some kind of soulmates, you are more like twin flames, entwining eternally; you have an intuitive understanding of one another, I believe; and you know between you there is, and always will be, the way of tenderness.

"I am sorry, Ning, maybe I am upsetting you. Anyway, by the time you get this letter, I will probably be dead. For

a long time now, I have had pains inside. The herbalist and acupuncturist can make one comfortable, but not stave off the Grim Reaper for ever. I am so weak now, I know the end is not far away.

"But I want you to know, Ning, my darling son, I nursed you at my breast for two years, like a proper Chinese mother. I watched you crawl, then totter your first steps on your feet, then run about with the chickens in the yard, bare-bottomed and dusty. I had you snatched from me and taken away to a far land so that I was not able to see you grow and mature. But I was blessed that you returned to me, in my final years, a fine, decent, strapping man.

"I want you to know, I have faith in you. You are not a bad person. You have been served an injustice, but sure isn't that often the way of the world, of this wretched life? What matters is how we face our travails, how we look them in the eye and not be bowed by them. And though others may doubt your word, not trust your innocence, they cAnot be blamed for what they believe when they do not possess the full facts and so, I hope, dear Ning, you can accept their suspicion without blame or resentment, make allowance for it, for it is only human to react that way. They have suffered a loss, which has to be taken into consideration. You have had to wait, my boy, for justice, and I fear you may not receive it until the next world rather than get it in this one. But if that is the case, know that I will be there waiting for you with open arms, to share the time with you which I was so cruelly deprived of in this life.

"These long months incarcerated may have taken their toll on your spirit, sapped your will to believe in all that is good and true and worthy; but I implore you not to lose faith – faith in the veracity of your destiny. I sense there is some great reckoning due to you and that it will come, somehow, some time. I hope you receive it in this world. There is some great drama left to be played out for you, though I cAnot tell what it may be nor will I ever be there

173

to witness any further part of your voyage forth. But where you will walk, whether it be to the wharf again, or along some paradisiacal lane with a beautiful companion, or be it slow, sad steps to a menacing gallows, be assured my spirit will walk with you, in love and pride.

"Your adoring mother, Fen."

Nathan's tears caused more blurring of the ink lines, in places where hers had failed to spot.

Chapter 22

Jilin, Summer, 1779

Ju was on stage at Jilin's Imperial Theatre. She was the lead in a musical show. The stage was vast, framed with luxurious red velvet curtains, tasselled with gold braid, the boxes and balconies decorated with the finest stucco, just like any European theatre. It was different from Peking's Celestial Theatre only in size.

Tonight was special, for Dewei had brought their mother as a treat, with Mei and her husband there, as Hua was babysitting for them. After the show, Ju changed and met them next door, at the Imperial Hotel's dining room.

They chatted happily for some time, until Ju noticed her brother was out-of-sorts. "What's wrong, Dewei?"

He eventually confessed, "I'm annoyed by that Boston man's presence. Him over there. Don't you know who he is?"

He was dressed in an ordinary suit, not a uniform. They did not recognise him.

"He was at the court. He's one of the captains of those Gray's ships. Imagine letting traders like that in a respectable place like this."

When Ju stared at Richard Hume, he sensed that animal instinct of being watched and turned, caught her eye. He knew who she was. He could tell she knew who he was, so he diverted his gaze, made a point of not looking at them again.

Mei's husband Yong asked, "Whatever happened to that man who killed Jia, anyway?"

Dewei said, "He was gaoled and sentenced to be executed. I am not often here in Jilin, so I went to the gaol to ask had the execution been carried out. They're doing it tomorrow morning."

Dewei told them how, yesterday morning, while they were still sleeping in their rooms at Ju's mansion outside the town, on this special trip arranged by Ju, he had woken and gone for a walk. He found the sign for the prison and walked in that direction. There it was, after an hour. So he went to the gate and asked to speak with the governor. They were so surprised by such a visit, the guards showed him in. There were few inmates awake, but the couple that were hanging out their bars watching his every move and trying to overhear the conversation, wolf-whistled him as he walked by.

The guard with him slammed his stick against the nearest iron bars. As they reverberated he screamed, "Down, you dogs!" He told Dewei, "They're just having a joke. Don't be intimidated."

Dewei was shown in to the functional office. The governor came in.

"Can't you sleep, boy? Coming here at this time?"

"Actually, yes, that's right."

"Who are you, what do you want? Jia's son, he said. We've no convicts of that name here at present that I can think of."

"My father was a victim. I am from Songhua. He was killed by the *fanquis*, Gray. He's supposed to be caged here like the animal he is."

"Oh, my boy, I'm so sorry. Yes! The flowery-flag devil, he's here still."

"He was sentenced to be executed."

"Well, there have been appeals. But the appeal process is now at an end. The Emperor was asked for clemency, but the Palace said there have been no new grounds for such an appeal, no new reason to compel His Majesty to rescind a legitimate court order."

"So, when does he die?"

The governor sighed. "Thursday."

"How come Thursday?"

"Executions here are always on Thursday. For a while, I must confess, we have been lapse in carrying it out. The man has a rich English family, they send money, food, drink. The guards keep most of it for themselves, don't want that to end. But you are quite right, the murdering swine should have been put to death by now. I'll see to it this week. How do you want it done?"

"How do you usually do it?"

"It depends on the crime. Stoning for rapists and perverts is popular. Sometimes we take them to the quarry where the hard labour is done and crush them by toppling big rocks on them. But that's unpleasant clearing up the mess, once the rock is broken, and there are few big enough ones now. There's always suffocating in an ash pit, live burial, or garrotting, boiling or disembowelment and dismemberment."

"Aren't they a bit quick?"

The governor nodded. "Look, we haven't done it for a long time but, since he was a European, and he threw your father down from a balcony in the drum tower, how about crucifixion? We can hang him up in the yard, choke him, and let him dangle there all weekend. It would be a message to the other inmates, who are being a bit unruly at the moment."

"Sounds the business to me."

"Once again," the governor told him as he walked him to the gate, "I'm sorry we haven't got round to that one yet."

"That's alright, I understand," Dewei told him. "A least now I know it will be done."

When Dewei had told his family the story of his visit to the gaol, taking a sip of wine, Mei said, "I know he was responsible for Daddy's death, but we were away home, didn't really take in anything about the court hearing. I always thought he was being prosecuted for carelessness, not murder. I don't see how that was possible, when it was an accident."

"What do you mean?" Ju asked.

"We were there, on the balcony, remember, Yong? With Gui's brothers? They were drunk, yahooing, had spilt beer all over the balcony floor. Remember, I slipped, too? Only you caught my arm …"

"Your buttock, as I recall, Mei darling! You wrapped your arm round the balcony railing."

"Anyway, Daddy slipped. The Boston fellow didn't push him, that was just one of Kun's drunken sons letting off steam. He reached out, tried to grab Daddy, but it was too late, he'd already taken the tumble."

Ju pointed at Mei, then at Yong. "Is this right?"

178

Yong nodded. "Oh yes. He slipped, I remember that clearly. Didn't everyone see that?"

Dewei grumbled, "Doesn't matter what happened, it's all that Boston bastard's fault. If he hadn't bothered Daddy there, he wouldn't have fallen."

"But it wasn't *murder*. It was an accident. You can't just execute him for an accident."

Yong shrugged his shoulders. "The court convicted him. It's too late now. Besides, he's just a Boston trader."

Dewei said, "Accident, deliberate, he killed Daddy."

Heng stared at her daughters, "It does sound like it wasn't malicious, as we all thought at the time. It's a bit harsh to execute him, but he was reckless, as Dewei says."

"But this changes everything!" Ju argued.

"Don't you start going soft on him again," Dewei exclaimed, "just because you know now he's to die at dawn."

Ju stood up, leaned with her knuckles on the tablecloth, staring at each of them in turn. "I hate the fact that Daddy's dead. If I thought Ning murdered him, I would let him be executed. Till now, I thought that was the case. But, it's clear that's not so. He is an innocent victim of an unfortunate misunderstanding. Do you not think if it was you, Dewei, who was on trial for his life, you might want justice, when it was an accident?"

Dewei nodded meekly.

Yong sipped wine. "Too late."

Ju stared at Mei. "Are you sure?"

"Of course ..."

"Are you willing to swear a binding legal oath about it?"

"If needs be. But, Ju ..."

Ju began moving away from the table. "Come on."

"What?" Mei asked.

"I know a lawyer. We're going to his house."

Yong protested, "It's late."

"It'll be too late to do the right thing if we don't get moving."

Ju led her sister and brother-in-law to an attorney's house, only a few minutes' walk away.

When he had welcomed the famous singer and her companions into his house, and heard the story, he said, "You realise, if we make representation to a judge tonight, it will be most unusual, coming from the family of the victim, who are usually the first to clamour for the execution?"

Mei agreed with Ju now, "We have to do the right thing."

"And your brother?"

"He will come round in time," Ju said.

"And your mother?"

"She's in agreement."

So the lawyer drew up the legal petition and went with them to the judge's house. The story was told again. He sat for some time, deliberating about the matter. He stared into space. When he did finally turn to them, it was to say, "Your new evidence is sufficient to permit a stay of execution. He will have to remain in gaol until there is another hearing. In a week or so. This will carry and he will be released. How do you feel about that, that the supposed killer of this man, your father, will walk free?"

Ju said, "If he's innocent of any crime, so he should."

"Are you sure about this?"

Ju nodded.

"What new evidence is there?"

Ju told him of Mei's and Yong's recollection.

Guards were walking Nathan out from his cell to the yard where the huge post stood ominously. Some locals had gathered, for it was a public execution. They were still drunk from the night before. They were cackling, jeering as he was led out, and spitting crumbs as they nibbled at bread rolls or cakes they had brought with them. Nathan carried the crossbeam on his shoulder. A rotten fruit splatted on it, spots stung his eye, dirtied his face. The beam was chafing his skin. In his mind, he felt calm.

But he snapped at his guards fiercely, "This is sacrilegious, you damn, ignorant coolies!"

The guard nearest him whacked him with his truncheon-like stick and spat in his face. The crowd roared.

"I'm no saint or Son of God, I'm just an ordinary man, how dare you do this," he protested. "It's a mockery. Christ said, *forgive them, they are just heathens, they don't know what they're doing.* But let me tell you, God will have His vengeance on you for this. Have you had the decency to provide me with a minister?"

Ignoring his hostility, the guards placed a hood over his head, rather than a crown of thorns, as they prepared the crossbeam. They had him dump it on the ground, they shoved him down to his knees and onto his back, so his hands could be tied to it. They arranged it on ropes and pulleys. They positioned it ready to hoist him up once he was secured to the crossbeam. They began securing one wrist with hammer and nails, so that he squealed involuntarily, his high-pitched wail reverberating around the prison so that other inmates clapped their hands over their ears.

The governor came marching out from his office. The lawyer and Ju had moved away, got back in their carriage and headed to her country home by the time the drums fell silent, the hood was released and the wide-eyed Nathan was told of the last minute intercession. Ju heard only a faint wail, did not realise the source.

Nathan tried to stand, clutching his bleeding wrist, which the warden himself had wrenched from the iron spike, but he dropped to his knees on the hard, stony ground, moaning with agony. His trousers were soiled. He sobbed, uncontrollably.

As his arms were freed the crowd began to scream obscenities at the guards for depriving them of a spectacle. The governor barked orders to his men and two ran inside, then came hurrying out, dragging Bao. They passed by one another as Nathan was escorted back to his cell by wide-eyed, bemused guards. He stared at Bao in horror.

Bao just grinned back and said to him, "Well, tell me about this god of yours, white man. Because I could do with one of these miracles, too."

Nathan was in too much pain to snap at them anymore, except for trying to say to the guard who had hit and spat on him, "I'll get you some night in a backstreet, you coolie bastard!" The fellow did not hear him clearly, through his gasped pain.

Just as Nathan was reaching the iron-barred gate back into the prison building and the wooden door beyond, something struck him on the back. Thumps ricocheted off the wall above and beside him. He was able to see over his shoulder that the crowd were lifting stones from the yard and throwing them. Only a few had targeted him, however: Bao was the main focus of their wrath. The guards had abandoned Bao amidst the volley of rocks raining down on him, pushing him down onto the crossbeam as they retreated. He never got up, the assault was so intense.

As the people were there expecting a culmination, they could not just let Bao hang around for too long, slowly slipping away. So the governor drew his ceremonial sword, beckoned them to desist, which the crowd did. The governor slit Bao's throat, more as a signal of finality than a *coup de grace* or insurance. At the sight of the first gush over the shirt and spatter onto the dusty ground, the crowd wailed with wicked joy. Bao satisfied their bestial need by groaning loudly, whether it was a rush of lung air or actual last breath was unclear.

The governor barked at the spectators, "Right, that's it, folks. Show's over." The guards ushered them to the front gate.

Nathan lay on the straw most of the day, exhausted. He heard the swish of shovels as inmates dug a hole by the wall. He heard the *poof* of lime being tossed in, then the thumps as the earth was returned, to cover the grim deposit.

When his food was brought that night, there was a little extra for Nathan. The guard had to shake him to rouse him to come eat.

"What's done is done, no point in your letting yourself fade away. You'll be out soon. It's for a reason, isn't it?"

Nathan stared at the clanging cell door. He rolled over, hoisted himself to his feet, seized his food and ate. Stared at the cell bars again, wondering.

Chapter 23

Jilin and Canton, Summer, 1779

Within a week, Nathan was released. The governor ensured that week that Nathan received as much food and wine as his belly could cope with. His exercise regime had kept him fit, the additional rations helped fill him out somewhat.

The guard who had hit him and spat in his face in the yard appeared the evening before his last in the gaol. He left the cell door open behind him, stood square before him, legs apart, stick in hand, staring at him. Nathan sat back, stared up at him. After an age, the guard swivelled on his heels, slowly walked out, closing the cell door behind him.

The evening before he was due to be released, An appeared at the gates. Adam Gray had sent him to wait for Nathan's freedom and to accompany him to Jilin City. The warden was still at the gaol. He despatched a messenger to the magistrate's house. The paperwork was ready, had come back from Peking that afternoon. He was going to check it and complete the bureaucracy in the morning. But since the messenger was sent, he went to the office, checked the papers, stamped and signed the release papers, handed them to the messenger. An was sitting with the warden, it was nearly midnight when the messenger returned. A guard unlocked the cell, Nathan was brought from his dozing on straw to the exit, handed his copy of the release document and shown to the gate.

"My chop!" he joked to An as they walked down the road from the gaol.

"It's a long walk to the town, but there's a tavern on the outskirts we can rest at."

Nathan was holding his arms out, as if embracing the stars. "I can feel the breeze, taste the fresh air, see such wide space, it's amazing! This is wonderful! Freedom! Worth waiting for. I don't care how long we walk, I could walk forever."

When they reached the tavern, it was late, the local drinkers had all gone, the innkeeper was tidying up. He gave them a beer each and some bread and chicken, told them there was a room.

When they had eaten and had the beer, Nathan began to wilt. They went to the room. An took up most of the mattress, but Nathan did not care, he was on a soft mattress, not a layer of fusty straw. He was soon asleep and did not waken until late morning.

An had been up, eaten, taken a stroll, sat and chatted with the innkeeper as he prepared for the lunchtime crowd. Nathan was so late rising, he and An had lunch. As they sat down to a meal of rice and steamed vegetables, Nathan recalled the times he had sat in taverns in various ports with his fellow officers, to have a similar meal. But none before tasted as exquisite as this meal.

Nathan took some time to himself. He hired a carriage and disappeared. An wondered was he visiting some woman. Nathan never told anyone that he was driven to a village not far away, found the most ramshackle cottage there. A few locals saw him arrive, pretended he was invisible as he went into the house. But he was only a few moments, not an hour, so they were quizzical. None were more bemused than the whippet-like woman who dwelt there.

When her neighbour appeared at the door, as the carriage was over the crest of the hill, to ask, "Is everything alright?" she told her, "He said he knew Bao. He gave me this, for my trouble." She showed the neighbour a shiny silver coin. She did not show the neighbour the other coins, which she hid, her heart singing, knowing how long she was going to be secure now.

An arranged for passage on a junk from Jilin to Canton. Nathan stood on deck with the wind on his face, the salt water stinging his lips and throat, the coastline constantly in view making him feel so nostalgic for the times they had plied this route in the *Firestorm*.

As they were past Hong Kong's peninsula and Macao was in sight, with its flurry of junks and ships, An asked Nathan, "So, sir, are you ready for more sea adventures on the *Firestorm*?"

"No more 'sir', An. Just call me Ning."

"Does that mean you have lost your yearning for the ocean?"

"Did I ever truly have it?"

"Well, I didn't. You know I've always wanted to be in the theatre. I keep trying, leaving it, going back to it. It chews me up and spits me out like an irritable dragon. Like a fool, I keep going back, trying to prod its backside with a field fork."

"You must be dedicated to it. You were made a eunuch so you could be a performer."

An laughed. "That was my stingy old father. He'd three daughters and six other sons and didn't want the bother of more grandchildren. Sold me off to an acting troupe, along with two pigs. Better if he'd gelded himself at my age than me!"

The junk only went as far as Macao Roads. The two sailors hitched a lift in a Hong merchant's carriage to Whampoa.

When the carriage turned a bend in the road and the *Firepower* and *Firestorm* loomed, silhouetted against the factory warehouses and the mountains beyond, with the bustle of dockers loading cargo on ships and moving supplies into sheds, Nathan sobbed. He waited until he had control of himself again before he stepped out of the carriage. The hoppo shook hands with him, looking away in embarrassment.

An walked with Nathan across the wharf to the storage house. Adam was there, listening as Josias and the chop house official went through a list of goods. He hugged his boy. Nathan let the old fellow hold him for as long as he needed to. They were all speechless.

Josias broke the marvel by asking, "Come aboard, Nathan?"

He shook his head. "Let's go to a hotel."

Adam nodded. It was evening. They went to the nearest inn. An ensured there was a room for Nathan, then left the officers dining and drinking.

Josias told him, "We are actually due to sail next week. Richard and I take the ships back to Boston. Your father has stayed here all this time, awaiting this day."

"Or last week's," Nathan said, meaning an execution.

"I have prayed to God for your deliverance."

"I'm sure most fathers do," Nathan replied.

"You got a miracle, didn't you, you ungrateful cur!" Josias Foster suddenly turned on him. Josias stood up. He recovered his dignity immediately, said to Nathan, "Forgive me, sir. It has been a difficult time for all of us. I am forgetting it has been hardest on you, yourself. Your mood will be due to what you have been through. But I think it best you have some time alone with your father. Excuse me, gentlemen." With that, Josias walked swiftly away.

Adam did not refer to the incident. He stared at Nathan. Nathan was silent for a time.

"Well, you can rest up for a few days, enjoy stretching your legs. Tidy yourself up," Adam said, eyeing the queue. "Then we can go home."

"I am home."

"I beg your pardon?"

"China is my home."

"Boy, the authorities don't want you here, any more than we want you here after what happened to you. Once you're back in Boston, you can run operations from there. And I shall remain at home from now on, too. Your brothers are old enough to accompany the ships on voyages in the future. And the young fellows, Foster and Hume, can take over the captaincies for now. Joseph wants to retire, too."

"I never felt I belonged there. America. For all its beauty and wondrousness. And despite what has happened here, despite what she has done to me, I *love* China. I will not leave her."

"Her? You talk as if a lump of rocks was a woman. Oh, is that it, the girl? She's long gone! Probably married by now, with half a dozen brats swinging off her skirts. Even if you did escape the crucifix, you caused her father's death. Do you think she'll ever forgive you? They say she went to the prison with the pardon, to save you, and maybe she did, but she didn't hang around to see you, or come to meet you when you got out, did she?"

"It's not even about Ju. It's me, me." He placed a hand at his breastbone.

188

Adam Gray dropped his chopsticks on his plate in disgust. "Have I wasted two years of my life agonising over a prodigal son who won't even acknowledge the error of his ways when he reaches rock-bottom, but is prepared to sink even lower, sink himself completely in the mire, is prepared to compound his foolishness even further? Ah!" He rose to his feet. "Well, if you come to your senses, you know where we are, Nathaniel. I love you so dearly, it breaks my heart to hear you talk this way. But you are a grown man, you have to make your own choices and, even, mistakes. You're a desperate fellow! I hope you will join us when we sail next week. Or if not, I will be waiting at home, 'til my dying day."

He was shaking with emotion. Nathan rose as he was about to walk away. "I don't hate any of you. I love you all. It's not foolishness to - to follow my own destiny. I know you can't see my life, my passion is not ships and stock and cargoes and trade. I admire you more than any man alive. I envy you: your luck and skill in business, your steadfastness of purpose, your decency and integrity, all that you are – God how I wish I could be like you. But I'm not, father. I - I'm not sure what I should be doing, yet. All I know is, deep in my gut, this is my home, and this is where I belong. I can't go back to Boston. Though I will miss you all, you and mother, and all my siblings, and friends …"

"And fiancée? You have a duty to her."

"Would she want me now? Would she not always live in dread of me? Wonder what is true? Because she has not been here, to know how it has been? I know we would live in embarrassment. I cannot thrust that upon poor Martha. She is kind and decent, but she is not quite right for me. Nor I for her."

Adam sighed deeply. He nodded. "I see that, for now, you need to recover from your ordeal. Okay, so, you are safe and free now. Please stay that way. Let us meet every day until we sail. If you still feel you cannot come with us, then I shall return to our family. Say you are recovering. That you are overseeing operations at this side for now. Perhaps you will return in due course. Leave the gate open. I will offer Miss Alexander her freedom. She will refuse, I know. But the time will come when she will, through her father's and my guidance, choose a different mate. She has waited long enough, we cannot have her live in false hope. But I will always live in hope, neither false nor unrealistic, but paternal and charitable."

They shook hands and he left. Nathan sat down, finished his meal, and then returned to the hotel to rest.

On the way, he saw a shape curled up on the pavement by a shop doorway. As he passed, it unwound, the wizened face stared out from the shawl at him. "Nathan-yel."

He stopped in his tracks. "You."

"Well, what of my predictions? The rain alight, on fire? A dark room and rebirth?"

He thought for a moment, then nodded. "Good, very good. What next, my dear, since I am down on my luck, freshly reborn into this world with little to show for myself and few prospects that *I* can see ahead?"

She got her metal bowl, poured water into it from a jug, set it rippling, then studied it intently. "You did not marry yet?"

"No. Who would have a wretch like me?"

"Oh ye of little faith – know that there is positive change ahead. Know that you will receive the happiness and love that you deserve. The one that you have been wanting to be with will give you all that you crave."

"I doubt that, I doubt I'll ever see her again."

The crone shook her head adamantly. "Await divine timing. What is desired will be made manifest. Wealth, comfort of living in a tranquil place, by an expanse of water. A separation will be healed; you are the only one close to her heart. You will meet again soon. It will be. Spirit is adamant."

"Well, I can't see it, but thank you."

Nathan dropped three coins into the old woman's lap. She cackled as he walked on, towards his lonely hotel room.

Nathan shook hands with his father again at the harbour wall the day the *Firepower* and *Firestorm* sailed. When the gangplank was raised, his father saluted him from the deck, then went below immediately. Nathan stood on, until the two ships were so distant on the Pearl River they could no longer be discerned.

When he turned to leave, he saw An loitering at the warehouse corner. He walked over to him.

"Spying on me?"

"Just seeing if you went or really stayed."

"In order to report to whom?"

"No one. Out of personal curiosity. Why, you think I am sent to see by Ju? Or someone?" He shook his head. "You haven't asked about her in all this time."

"She's not here, is she?"

"She's in Peking again, the latest stage in her stint at the Celestial Theatre. A show with her songs in it. She knocks 'em dead!"

"Why don't you go join the troupe?"

"Performers like me are ten-a-penny."

"But it might as well be you in that line-up as anyone else."

"I'll have another go soon. Maybe for now I should stay with you."

"Keep me out of trouble?"

An shrugged his shoulders. "Just to see you settled back into life outside four walls."

"You appoint yourself my nanny?"

"A friend, I hope. Well, sir, I mean, a servant."

Nathan nodded. "I'm sorry, I don't mean to sound abrupt. Yes, maybe I do need a nanny for a time. Well, An, I don't know about you, but I have been out of prison for a week and done nothing but eat and sleep. Now, I am revived. And restless. After two years in a hellhole. And lately having faced death. Ah, I am alive! So, let's go find ourselves an afternoon of debauchery in some opium den, and worry about business for Gray and Sons Imports and Exports tomorrow!"

Chapter 24

Canton, Summer, 1780

Nathan busied himself trading out of the factories at Whampoa. He would buy a raw commodity, ship it and sell it on. As well as earning enough to live on, he was able to bank some money for the family firm. He wrote to Boston with every ship leaving for Massachusetts. He would dine at the *Inn of a Thousand Faces,* drink only a very little, never seek solace in an opium pipe.

After watching the singers performing, Nathan would ask them who they had toured with, where, hoping to hear some news of Ju. And he did hear of her occasionally: how she was on an extended run at the Celestial Theatre in Peking, off for a short tour north, or west, or east, then back to the Celestial Theatre, where she was always the star turn.

To begin with, the local girls would tempt him. One in particular tried her luck, sitting beside him at his table as he ate, sharing a beer. She took his rough hand, guided it beneath the table, and placed it on a warm inner thigh. Ning lifted it back to his knife, to slice some beef.

"You are very lovely," he told her, "but I am waiting for someone."

The girl looked round her, got up and left him. She sat on a stool at the bar that quiet evening, sipping her drink. When Ning was almost finished his meal and no one came, she tried again.

"She has stood you up."

"Patience is a virtue."

"I've no patience!"

"I didn't mean she was necessarily coming tonight. A prophetess told me it is not the end between us, you see? I may have a long wait." He stood up, throwing his money on the table.

"Then why not wait with me?" She grabbed his arm, swinging against him.

Now and again, Peng would perform at the *Inn of a Thousand Faces*. Nathan would never speak with him. He would observe the singer joking with the other performers, charming the female fans. Nathan would leave once Peng began his set.

At last, An was back. He and Ai were actually singing in a short comedy musical play that was touring. A bawdy version of *Aladdin*. An was big and had his distinctive high voice, thanks to his status as a eunuch, so he was a popular solo act and drag queen, in his role as Empress Tun-chi, queen of the Peking laundrette. Ai was the star, as Aladdin. An spotted Nathan and, after the show, went out to the audience to speak with him.

"You've hit the big time, An! Marvellous show!"

"You're too kind, sir."

"Ning, now. No airs and graces for me."

"After this run, I will likely be back to stagehand, but I don't mind. It's nice to perform and to support. Ai is the real star."

"She certainly is! Have you seen Ju recently?"

"You still think about her? I think she burns in your heart."

"Is she in Peking?" he asked, avoiding a confession.

An nodded. "She's only got a few one night shows in other places, over the next six weeks or so. I will be back there myself, in a few weeks' time. The grand finale of our tour – imagine, big clumsy An, hoofing it in the Celestial Theatre in Peking! I can die happy once that is achieved! But how are you doing, all alone in Canton?"

"I am not alone. Li left the ship, is my servant. Cooks for me. I have made friends with the Hong merchants, hoppos and chop officials. When Boston men come in to Whampoa, they meet with me. I have so many trade contacts now. It's a roaring trade, being a middle man."

"But you are alone. It's not good for a man to be alone. When he's settled, no longer a sailor. You should think about establishing a family."

Ning's face expanded with surprise. "I haven't thought about anything like that!"

An stood up to go. "Our friends will want me to go for a meal with them. Will you join us? There are quite a few attractive dancers in the troupe."

Ning grinned. "I know I sound like a boring old fart, but I'm not in the mood, sorry."

"I understand. I once felt deeply for someone. When it was not possible to be together, for such a long time, I could not muster the enthusiasm to … party. Now, my heart is healed, the scar can barely be seen or traced. I can be merry again. Someday, you will be at ease within your skin again, Ning, my friend."

He laughed. "That depends on circumstances."

"Sir," An said, leaving, "You've got it bad."

"I've got nothing!" he shouted across the tavern. And waved a hand, dismissing his protests.

Chapter 25

Peking, Autumn, 1780

The trees were golden brown and red-leaved, or bare and strewn with carpets of russet and gold as Nathan travelled from the port to Peking's bustling centre. He had completed his business at the wharf, having sailed on a friendly merchant's vessel from Canton. He was affording himself some time to see the capital for the first time.

A local guide showed him the wall of the Forbidden City. From a hilltop, they got a better view. He stayed overnight in a hotel. He went that evening to the Celestial Theatre.

Ning saw all the acts, but it was the star turn singer among the variety acts he was interested in seeing. Waiting, he was unemotional. Even seeing her spotlit, hearing her voice meant little: she was someone else on stage. Her songs were uplifting, up tempo ones full of *joie de vivre*.

Then, she sang a ballad about being engulfed by fire, but being saved. Tears welled in his eyes. Ning fought back his sensitivity. He smiled broadly to see Ju receive such an ovation, the raucous encore she deserved.

When the show ended, he made his way to the stage door and waited nearby, hidden in shadows but able to see who came and went. He wondered who would meet her – anyone? A carriage drew up and he thought he saw Gang leave, someone with him, reckoned that must have been her.

Walking back to his hotel, he remonstrated with himself in his head: should I have gone over, introduced myself? Should I have? But she's never contacted me in all this time, why bother? It was her last night in the show for some time, am I a fool not to have taken the opportunity, to at least try?

The next day, he went to the carriage station to take his booked transportation back to the port. He was there early. The carriage was nowhere to be seen, was late coming from the harbour.

And there was Ju. Slightly older about the face, but the same Ju. Well dressed, in a beautiful frock, parasol in hand, lace gloves, like a proper lady.

"What are you doing here?" he asked her without thinking, having marched over the few paces to where she was.

Ju turned, started to see him there. Her eyes smiled as she replied, "Oh, I'm getting a carriage back to Jilin. My show run has ended. I hardly recognised you, with your queue and everything." She looked him up and down, taking in his Manchu dress.

"Don't you have your own carriages?"

"I did have for a while. Yong ran that venture for me. But they're too expense to run. It wasn't much of a money-spinner. How did you know that?"

"An must have told me. The sensible country girl in you, saving every penny! Doesn't Gang work for you now, why's he not here to look out for you?"

"Yes, he does work for me, but he's not coming, he's got a week off now. How did you know that?"

"An must have told me!"

"How is your spy An? I haven't see him for a while."

Ning grabbed a passing carriage driver by the arm, asked when his and Ju's carriages would be ready. They were told not for an hour, they were running late.

"Typical," he remarked. "Perhaps we should wait in that tea shop, get a cup?"

Ju nodded and walked with him.

"An's grand! No different. Pleased as punch to have been so high up the billing in a show. You know An, content with his lot. He works for me, now. No more sea for him, he's my Gang."

She laughed and nodded. They ordered tea and sweetmeats. "How time has flown since we were kids practising music in Songhua's drum tower."

"I should thank you for saving my life," he said awkwardly. "Words cannot express the gratitude ..."

She shook her head. "It was the right thing. You should be free. Why are you in China? Why are you not in Boston? Have you been home and come back? I suppose you are married now ..."

"No. I never went back."

"Never? Why not, Ning?" Her hand rested on his for a moment. Their eyes met. Neither looked down at the hand nor reacted to the touch.

"I like China!" he laughed.

"I don't understand how you could stick the place after what you went through!"

"Gaol I didn't like. But it could be a gaol anywhere." After a pause, he added, "And I have yet to apologise, to express my condolences on your father's death ..."

She shook her head, looked away. Stirred her tea. "It wasn't your fault."

"I think so."

She stared into his eyes.

"So do you."

She was silent for a moment. "Sometimes. But it was mine, too, in a way. And other people's. And his own, for losing his temper. And no one's. Who knows. It can't be changed, that's all."

"Well, it plays on my mind."

"That's understandable, since you were nearly executed and spent so long in prison. I am coming to terms with it. Only recently, really. Sometimes the second year of grief is worse than the first."

He nodded. "Fen died. While I was in prison. She wrote to me." He touched his breast, to signify the letter was in his inside pocket.

Ju nodded. "I visited her when I could, as she was ailing. We didn't always see eye-to-eye, but she was always kind to me."

"I was wrong about her – for all her struggles, compromises, she had a kind heart."

Ju nodded, almost weeping. "She was good."

They talked about her shows, Ning's fledgling chandler's business, and his trade with and for other Boston merchants, his representing his family firm on a permanent basis in Canton. An's antics. Li's notorious benders. Ning's occasional business trips to Dandong and Jilin.

"What about Gui?" he ventured.

She shrugged her shoulders. "Sometimes our paths cross. He plays with his friends in their band, still. He just likes to play his music, that's all. He has a steady woman. They have a little boy, so cute!"

"You live not far from the gaol in Jilin, don't you?"

"Yes. A beautiful location, private, with a view from the hills over the coast, yet secluded. You should come and see it. Some friends visit me, my sister Mei is quite close, my nephews and nieces come and stay when she and Yong want a break from them! My mother lives with me, now. And Hua will live in the house next to us, when she marries. Dewei lives at home in Songhua, farms, grows tea. Finest pekoe, some congo, some souchong. Only the best, now. We visit him a couple of times a year. I bought Madame Lihwa's smallholding and tavern when she died. I guess I will have to get them fixed up, they are in need of some love. Where I am in Jilin … well … I will tell you more … some time …"

As their conversation faded, their eyes met. Behind them somewhere, a driver was calling: the carriage to the harbour, which Ning would be sharing, crammed in with several other passengers. He waved, to show he was coming. He drained his tea cup, then stood up. He was about to bow, in departure, but Ju got to her feet and walked with him to the carriage. He threw his bag on the roof and turned to face her.

"It's been wonderful to see you again," he said.

Ju nodded. "It's nice to see you again, Ning. I'm glad we bumped into one another. Do come and visit. I am at home in Jilin for the rest of the year. To rest. Spend time with mother, because she is ailing. And to write some new songs!"

Ning nodded. "I will. As soon as I get back to Canton and get things sorted, in a few weeks, I will have a trip to Jilin to do, actually. So, I can inspect this mansion of yours!"

"It's hardly a mansion! Well …"

"Though I'm hardly Mister Life-and-soul-of-the-party. I'm a bit of a dead fish these days."

"I'm no party animal myself. I lead a quiet life. Mostly work. Yes, do come to the house, near Jilin."

"As long as I don't take a wrong turn and end up in the gaol house again! There's at least one guard there wants to pummel me."

"Why?"

"Because I'm a Boston man. Because I gave him such lip when he was marching me off to crucify me."

"Well, that's understandable."

"Forgivable? You would say that, you're so - kind."

She laughed and reached up, touched his face with her warm, soft hand, and kissed him. Ning melted into the kiss, held on as long as possible. She was such a beautiful kisser. His mind swirled. He was recalling the first time they kissed.

When they broke apart at last, she hugged him. He whispered something in her ear, which, though Ju strained to hear it, she just could not make out. But his breath brushed her neck, causing goosebumps to ripple all along her flesh; her face and bosom blushed; a shiver rivuletted up her spine; and a flutter within her core seized control for a moment. And that made all the difference.

He climbed into the carriage. When he looked out of the open door, she was walking away. She did turn and wave, but she was far enough away not to catch his gaze directly. But he knew she was smiling.

As Ning's carriage sped away and she waited the few minutes until her own was ready to move off, Ju wondered about what she had just done. She was waiting in the carriage and the woman next to her, almost her mother's age, asked, in an incredulous tone, so that Ju was unsure whether she was just being curious or censorious, "Is that European fellow your lover?"

Ju said, "We are ... used to be friends."

"I've never had a European lover. Are they any good?"

"He's very kind," Ju replied politely.

"Ah! That's the only thing that matters. Money, looks, sense of humour, virility, and these things are all important, but they are useless if he's a rascal, a tyrant or a brute. And I should know. I've had three husbands, one of each, in that order. But, thank goodness, now I am a settled widow I have a lover who is *kind* and considerate."

"And rich, good-looking, funny and virile?" Ju laughed.

The woman stared at her in mock consternation. "Of course!" she laughed as their carriage sped off towards Jilin. "And younger!"

Chapter 26

Jilin, Early Winter, 1780

Ning had received a letter each week from Ju and had replied, since sending notice of the dates of his trip to Jilin City on business. He travelled there to conduct his business and was now satisfied with the outcomes. So he took a carriage and drove out to the gates of the gaol. Seeing the looming walls made his stomach churn.

"That's enough!" he called, banging on the carriage side, anxious to get away. The driver looked at him with sullen eyes, peeved that he was abusing his vehicle. He desisted from doing so, but thought to himself, if the fellow only knew what he had been through, in that place. How could he even suspect a Boston man had ever been an inmate there? It was unthinkable. For, despite his always wearing the local style now, and being swarthy, he was still clearly foreign.

They drove as far as the fork in the road, then he asked the man to stop. Now the driver truly did think him mad, for Ning wanted out, to walk, alone in this godforsaken place. But he was paid, so he rode off back to the city. And Ning was left to stroll the hour or so towards Ju's secluded mansion beyond the wooded drumlins. As he set out, Ning recalled the fortune teller's words about a road with a fork. He had been down the one to the prison, where would this other lead, he wondered. She had said one would be a longer road; he wondered had he been on the longer of the two already, or would this path lead to some convoluted destiny?

When Ning reached the place, he smiled to himself how it made him think of a replica Forbidden City, with all its separate compounds, or rooms. He heard a child playing nearby, passed across a garden towards an ornamental pond. He recognised Mei, watching over as their child splashed in the pond with a ball.

Heng saw him first. He bowed to her with the customary ritualistic grandeur. She bowed back.

"I must express to you my profound and sincere sympathy. Your husband's loss was unintentional."

"Sir, I am reconciled to my grief. What was done cannot be undone. You suffered as a consequence. If there was a debt to be paid, it has been paid."

He bowed again. "Your daughter has a beautiful home."

Heng tried to suppress a proud smile. "It always amazes me that the foolishness and self-indulgence of the damn theatres can result in such luxury."

"You disapprove of song and plays?"

"I am a country woman with no time for such frivolities. I spent my time rearing children, keeping house and helping in the fields." She held out calloused hands. "Ju keeps saying, 'times have changed'. To an extent, this may be true. All I know is, in my day the theatres and taverns were considered the hang-outs of drunkards, opium-eaters and whores. To be an actor was to be a dog;

to be an actress was to be a harlot." She shrugged her shoulders.

Ju was approaching from the house, with her brother-in-law. "Ning! I was discussing next season's cropping with Yong. He's the estate manager."

Heng said to them, "I have tired myself out. I will go for a lie down before dinner."

Yong swopped bows with Ning, then joined his family, played with the child in the water, throwing the ball to her. Ju walked with Ning along the gravel path, through some trees, to open parkland beyond.

"Why do you want to be Chinese?" she asked, flicking his queue playfully.

"Perhaps the half of the blood that is in me that is from my mother dominates?"

"How did your business trip go?"

"Excellently, thank you! You mother isn't enamoured with singers and actresses."

"You were talking. Was that awkward?"

"The ice is broken."

"If she cussed you for Daddy's death …"

He shook his head, laughing. "I must say, I was surprised. She has suffered much."

Ju took his arm, squeezed against him in gratitude. "We all have. It's in the past, now."

"And your future seems bright." He gestured around them, at the estate lands.

Ju scrunched up her nose. She sighed deeply. "Yong, Mei and Mum convinced me to buy this as an investment. We did get it cheap, the old master had drunk himself to death and gambled his family fortune away. It's okay as an enterprise for Yong and Mei, to keep them interested. And it is profitable. But the actual house," Ju flapped an arm, "it's just not me. Too ..."

"Rococo?"

She nodded, "Too grand for me. And just not the location I'm comfortable with."

"What would you prefer?"

"I'm not sure. The usual story, I know when I see it."

"Songhua, instead of Jilin?"

"I think so. Mum was glad to be here, away from there, after Daddy died. But who knows, maybe she would go back. Hua would rather be there. She's there at the moment, practising being married! Since Mum is here, and unable to keep an eye on her."

"Your mother is unwell, you said."

"Shortness of breath. Pains in her chest. Say, why don't you come with me to Songhua, check out this place of Madame Lihwa's I've bought? Then Yong can stay home with Mei awhile ..."

"I don't mind a trip there, but Ju, I'd be lynched."

She shook her head. "Not if you come with us. Maybe Mum would come, too. She's not that bad that she could not do that."

"Well, if you're sure."

They sauntered back towards the house. As they approached the end of the parkland, passing some bare fruit trees, a gong sounded: the cook calling them to their meal. They saw Mei, Yong and the child heading in, for the child to get dried and changed in time for dinner.

Nathan recalled walking with Martha Alexander. Boston had been slightly colder. But it was how he had felt inside that he was hoping to analyse. That formal expectation; this relaxed homeliness. He just was not sure which man he was: Nathan or Ning. But he felt before much longer he would find out.

While they were at dinner, after the kitchen servant had brought out the food to the table and left them for the evening, Ju announced to Heng, "I'm going to go to Songhua tomorrow."

"I thought we were going the day after?" Yong responded.

"I am free now, and I have decided to do so tomorrow."

"There's the meeting with the woodcutter, and the drainage job to check at the far end ..."

Ju waved a hand. "You can sort that without me. That's estate stuff. Ning will escort me, I'll be safe. But, perhaps Mother wants to come for a few days? See how Hua is?"

"Yes! You don't mind my tagging along?"

"You come, too," was all she said, lowering her head to her soup.

Mei gave Ju an angry look, but more out of surprise than disagreement.

After the meal, Yong sat discussing estate matters with Ning. The drainage that needed doing, what he was going to check. Mei busied herself putting the child to bed, then working on her embroidery. Ju sat listening to the men talking and playing cards with Heng. She had gone out of the room when Heng, Yong and Mei retired for the night. Ning had some beer left, sat on to sip it.

Ju reappeared. She snuggled down cross-legged on the cushion beside him, yawning and taking his beer. "You seem to be getting on alright with Yong."

"He with me."

"Boring you about drainage."

"It's interesting."

"Not to me!"

"You miss the company of singers and musicians."

"Yes. But." She shook her head. "As a woman, I am already too old for the big stage. Women my age are expected to perform the bawdy ditties, instead of the heartfelt ballads that girls get to sing."

Ning frowned. "Is work starting to dry up?"

She nodded. "Lucky I made the most of it when I could."

"And invested wisely."

"Aw, you're sweet." She hugged and kissed him, rising as she did so. She yawned again. "Well, see you in the morning. I'm wrecked."

With that, she swept off towards her bedroom, leaving Ning aglow inside. He finished his beer, then made his way towards the other rooms. He strayed towards Ju's, listened at the doorway. He could heard her snoring. He laughed and went to the guest room, lay on the mattress and slept like an emperor.

Ju was eating breakfast before Ning or any of the others appeared. She thought back to their meeting, how she had found the stranger so interesting. His positivity was admirable. Her father's death – the blame – the shame – the mess with Gui. She winced at the thought of it all. Ning being saved from execution – yet she could not face him, then.

He appeared, had sat down opposite her and was pouring them both some tea when she blurted out, "I just couldn't face you again, when you got out of gaol." She shook her head.

"I know. It takes time to get over these things." He nodded. "And you've a harder shell than most, for letting the pain seep away through."

"Where's the rain seeping through?" Yong, asked, appearing, catching the end of their conversation.

"Just hypothetically speaking," Ning replied.

"Metaphorically," Ju corrected him.

As the carriage turned a corner, Ju elbowed Ning. He opened his eyes, straightened himself from leaning against her. "Sorry."

He woke Heng. She looked up through tired eyes.

Ju pointed out the window. Ning put his head out so he could see the road ahead. He recognised the drum tower, the familiar hills, the rows of tea bushes and rows of roofs. His heart juddered more surely than the carriage on the rough, country road.

"We'll go to the house, see Hua. Let Mum rest after the tiring journey."

He nodded.

When the carriage arrived, Dewei saw it from the fields and came to greet them. He had a young fellow with him.

Ning bowed to Dewei, but said nothing. Dewei bowed to him, saying, "It seems Tu Di Gong has spared you. Therefore, I must respect His wishes, and be respectful towards you."

"I will always be respectful towards you, Dewei," Ning replied.

"You pretend to be one of us?" Dewei pointed to Ning's queue and Chinese clothing.

"He is one of us," Ju told her brother.

"This is Mu, Hua's fiancé," he introduced his companion.

Ning bowed to Mu as Heng hugged Hua, who came running from the house.

"You're just in time to eat!" she said. "Does he have to be here?" she reacted hostilely.

Dewei told her, "I have come to realise it was an accident, as Mei said. If it was you or me who was in his position, would you want to be understood?"

"Ning spent two years in gaol for something he didn't do," Ju reminded her sister.

"It's alright," Ning said, looking at Hua, "I understand. You lost your father. Partly I am to blame."

"It was an accident," Ju snapped adamantly.

Hua nodded. "Well, anyway, you are all welcome to come and eat!"

During their meal, they all chatted and Hua seemed to accept Ning's presence more readily. He told them about his business in Canton, about trading in Jilin and other cities. Eventually, Heng excused herself, it was time for her afternoon nap. Dewei and Mu had work to do. Ning offered to help.

"You can help us tomorrow," Dewei told him. "We can cope alright today."

"Besides, I need you to go with me," Ju told him. She said to Dewei, "I have bought Madame Lihwa's estate. So, we can use the lands there, which march our own, to expand things from here!"

"Can we diversify? Grow rice, more grain?" Dewei asked excitedly.

Ju laughed. "Whatever you think is necessary!"

Excitedly, "Can we come tomorrow afternoon? If we get things finished here by lunchtime, with Ning's help, we can take a walk round later." Mu nodded vigorously in agreement.

"Of course!" Ju laughed.

She and Ning walked along the road to the road that wound round the lake. They reached the tavern first. They looked in. The staff were tidying up between busy times.

"Needs a lick of paint," she said.

"A complete refurbishment."

Ju nodded. "And a new name. A proper board, like the inns in the city. I don't want it to become known as Madame Ju's!" She thrust a hand to her mouth.

Ning laughed. "What about Madame Fen's? Or Madame Heng's?"

"Ah! Mother would kill me!"

"*The House of the Way of Tenderness*?"

She stared at him with incredulity. "That's lovely. Yes, I like that. It's fitting. For what I want. How did you come up with that?"

"Oh ..." he looked away.

"Is it a place in Canton?"

"No. You know the places in Canton. No. Just a phrase I heard once."

"I like it," she nodded. "Now, let's see the estate. And the house."

They walked the short distance towards Madame Lihwa's old home. On the way, Ju told Ning about the night Guan-yin had died out on the lake, how Gui and she had been brought here.

"Does it give you the creeps now?"

"No. Sorrow or joy are connected to an event itself, not necessarily to the place where it occurred."

"Does that stand for the drum tower, too?"

"We'll go there next. Yes, I know ... That's slightly different. Harder. We'll see."

They walked through the empty house. It was a manageable size comfortable, in need of a good clean but serviceable. I was a bright day and the sun blazed as the patio doors were opened and the light showered upon their shoulders and heads. They stepped across decking and the lawn, to a bench. They sat and admired the view of the lake.

"Madame Lihwa used to sit here for afternoon tea," Ju told him. "Admiring the view of the lake and trees. I think we should try again."

"Hm?" He took her hand in his. After a time, they turned to face one another, their faces moved together, lips met.

Ju felt her cheeks wet. As they parted for a moment, she discovered that Ning was sobbing. She held him close.

"What is it?"

"How can I be sure? This time you'll stay forever?"

"And I you? We don't know, do we?" She corrected herself, "I *do* know. It is forever, it is," she told him.

They kissed again, with renewed passion.

Chapter 27

Songhua Village, Jilin Province, China, November 1815

Ning's telling his tale of their lives to the bar servant Lan and to his drinking buddy Li was interrupted when Hai arrived in from the funeral event. Her husband Zan was with her and little Ya.

The child waved at him, calling, "*Ye-ye!*" to her grandpa as Hai took the child through to the back, to change her.

Lan got up from the seat and offered him a drink. Li waved for a refill.

Zan said to Ning, "Everyone is disconsolate. Especially poor Ai."

Ning nodded. "Li was saying how he's much older, yet he's still with us. Yet An is gone."

Zan gave them their beer. "So," she said to Ning, "you fixed up the house. It was the previous owner's? And this tavern. And here we are."

"A lifetime later," Ning acknowledged. "Dewei farms, Mu and Hua help him. As do I. Over near Jilin, Yong and

Mei run the big estate. We share. That's it. All the drama and adventures of youth long gone. The long, monotonous years of living and rearing a family are all that we have had since settling down in Songhua. Isn't that right, Li?"

The old sailor nodded. "No more oceans crossed, ports explored, theatres tried, only this tavern night after night, for years. At least Ju can enjoy the singing here, the music."

"Do you never see your own family, sir?"

"I travel occasionally to Canton. My nephews come there, to trade, the third generation of the family business. My brothers only came a few times. My *jiaren*, my true family is here," he said, as Ya gave a yell from out the back and Hai sushed her. To Li, he said, "After all Ju's touring and my sailing and trading, here we are, we found a short route by a long wandering, perhaps."

Li laughed. "Old Joseph used to say that! From Dorset, wasn't he?"

"That's right," Ning reminisced. "I forgot he was English, originally. He ended up in his wife's fishing village. Fishing, till their family were old enough to keep them."

When Hai came back out, she plonked the child on Zan's knee. "Mother's stirring."

"Dreaming? Or wakening?" his voice trailed, weakly.

Hai placed a hand on his. It was stone cold. "Are you alright, Daddy?"

"Fine," he said, slipping off his seat to the floor.

Hai fell to her knees, cradled his head. She pumped at his chest, tried to breathe air into his lungs. After a time, Li put a hand on her shoulder. Zan handed the child to Lan and took over. He looked up at Hai and Ju as she came in. He shook his head.

Ju knelt beside Ning and held his hand. "I'm here."

He whispered to her, "Others - meant nothing. With you, it has always been love."

"For me, too."

"Too much!" Hai gasped to herself.

His arm weakened and drooped. Lan worked a while longer on him. Ju touched Zan's shoulder, to let him know it was alright to stop. He sat back on his hunkers panting as she sat on the chair Ning had just been in.

"So it's all over now? One buried, another to join him so soon."

Hai was shaking. "What's happened him?"

Stoically, Ju told her, "His heart. Just like my mother."

They buried the Boston man up on the hilltop grave mound, beside his friend An. On his tombstone, Ju had engraved:

"And the sea will grant each man new hope,
As sleep brings dreams of home."
(*Christopher Columbus*)

The morning of the cremation rite, though, as Hai was helping Ju prepare him, she was straightening her father's jacket when, in the pocket she found a yellowing letter. The puzzled Hai placed it reluctantly in her mother's outstretched hand.

"Who was Fen? Sorry, I don't mean to upset you, Mother ..."

Ju laughed. Don't worry. She wasn't a concubine. Well, not of his, anyway. She was his birth mother."

"Really? How come I was never told any of this?"

Ju thought about it a moment and said, "Well, it was a long time ago. A different life."

216

Looking over her shoulder, Hai asked, "What does the letter say?"

Ju told her, "She wrote to him when she was dying, while he was in gaol."

"Daddy was in gaol? What for? Was he a swindler? Oh god!"

"No!" Ju laughed again. "They convicted him of murdering my father."

"What?! Why on earth?"

"My father wouldn't let us marry."

"So he killed him? All these secrets coming out now! Why couldn't it just be something ordinary, like a concubine!"

Ju shook her head. "I'll explain, sometime." She was reading the letter from Fen to herself. "I never knew he had this," she waved the letter. She read out to Hai, "Oh, look, Fen said of me, '*She is such a lovely girl.*' She was so kind." She read a little more, then murmured, "So that's where he got it from."

Hai took the letter and poured over it. "Wow." She read aloud, sharing with Hai, "Oh, listen - '*I sense there was a more cosmic connection between you than perhaps you even realise yourselves - I suspect, though your relationship with one another may be stormy at times, it will endure all hardships, any misunderstandings and disagreements, any separations however long, for you are so close to each other's hearts. You are both good, realistic people. Though others may seem to be important, caring, or some kind of soulmates, you are more like twin flames, entwining eternally; you have an intuitive understanding of one another, I believe; and you know between you there is, and always will be, the way of tenderness.*'

FINIS

217